Clandestinity

CLANDESTINITY

Antonio Moresco

Translated from Italian by Richard Dixon

DEEP VELLUM PUBLISHING

DALLAS, TEXAS

Deep Vellum Publishing
3000 Commerce St., Dallas, Texas 75226
deepvellum.org · @deepvellum

Deep Vellum is a 501c3 nonprofit literary arts organization
founded in 2013 with the mission to bring
the world into conversation through literature.

First Edition, 2022

ISBN (TPB) 978-1-64605-172-4 | ISBN (Ebook) 978-1-64605-173-1

Publication of this work supported by Perdrix Ventures.

Library of Congress Control Number: 2022932167

Front cover photo: *A man's head and shoulders, the right side of his face is contorted, 1864*, L. Haase.

Exterior design by Kit Schluter

Interior layout and typesetting by KGT

PRINTED IN THE UNITED STATES OF AMERICA

CONTENTS

The Blue Room

1

There were two doors into the house, one small and shabby at the top of some steps at the far end of the courtyard, the other very big, which led to a double stairway with a fake marble banister and a plaster bust at the top.

Two entrances, though each was also a double entrance. Thirty feet or so before the small door that led to the kitchen, there was another, flimsier wooden door with no lock. After the big door, on the other hand, at the top of the stairway was another door a good ten feet high and very heavy. This led to an enormous anteroom with no windows, poorly lit by an opaque skylight, blackened with dirt, that opened in the vaulted ceiling at the center of the room. The dim light that filtered in was enough to see the doors to the other rooms, some cupboards and benches, a large table with chairs around it, a shelf on which was one of the first models of television, a rack that held numerous walking sticks of all shapes (some hiding long blades that could be pulled out), and, lastly, right in front of the entrance door, an enormous cloak stand with coats piled one on the next, on top of which there was always a man's coat with an opossum collar, into whose soft fur, when no one could see him, he would bury his face, clasping it on either side.

As evening fell, all the doors into the house were barred, one after the other. First the door that led to the stairway, with panes of frosted glass, formed by four sections that swiveled open. Each section was covered by two movable panels, one outside and one inside, fixed by a series of hooks and bolts. Then the door at the top of the stairway, with its two locks and a sturdy chain. The small door on the steps could be closed by twisting a piece of wire around a rudimentary fastener that could also be opened from inside, whereas the kitchen door was bolted with a heavy bar inserted into two rings on either side of the door. Two small nails were dropped into small holes at each end to give added security to this curious locking system. During the day, the bar was propped against the wall beside the door. Sometimes, as he passed, he would take hold of it and swing it in the air.

The house consisted of two very different parts, so that one house seemed to be inside the other. Anyone who arrived from the main stairway, passing through the anteroom into the bedrooms and the dining hall, found themselves in a magnificent old mansion, though certain corners here and there showed signs of neglect and abandonment. But those who came in from the kitchen, who went past the bathroom and then along the narrow corridor as far as the anteroom, saw just a shabby old house. The corridor in particular gave this impression: much longer than normal, crossed high up by two iron bars, on which lay brooms and long bamboo poles used for cleaning the ceilings, with two large windows that looked out over the stairway. On opening them you could look down, as if from a precipice, at the first wide, low steps of the great stairway which, on visiting days, was covered by a red carpet, fixed at the base of each step by gold-colored rods that were carefully polished for the occasion.

There were many rooms and many people, and some entered the house from the stairway while others came up through the kitchen. He was sometimes amazed at the thought of living in a house like this and wandered the rooms as though he were seeing them each day for the first time. Through the anteroom, through his own room, which was a passageway with three doors, you arrived at another bedroom. Large oval pictures on its walls depicted battle scenes with cavalry. There was also a writing table and, farther away, a bureau. He took a key hidden in the belly of a lute and with this he silently opened the bureau. Inside were bundles of letters, a small pile of candies, a magnifying glass, a large block of chocolate with a corner missing, a knife with a handle, sticking out of which were tiny scissors and an amazing number of blades, a corkscrew, files, and other mysterious utensils. He bent down to look, fascinated. Having closed the bureau and returned the key to the belly of the lute, he opened the drawer of one of the cupboards: beneath a rolled-up rug there was a heavy sword whose blade was decorated almost to the tip, which was still slender and sharp. Beside the sword was a red velvet cap, which, according to someone in the house, had once belonged to Garibaldi. A hunting horn hung by one of the windows. He took it off the wall and traced its interminable spiral with his finger. He couldn't yet play it, he didn't have enough puff, nor did he know exactly what to do with his lips. But one day, after much perseverance, he had managed to play it: its extravagant sound had sown terror in every corner of the vast house.

Slowly he approached the center of the room, where an enormous bed stood on a wooden plinth. Around it were four columns that had once supported a canopy. He ran his hand over the gray fleece of the large sheepskin that covered it.

He left the room, returned to the anteroom, opened one of the doors to look at the stairway from above. He went into the dining hall, with its coffered ceiling and large portraits that hung from the walls. Then he opened a dark dresser full of doors, pulled out a crystal vase with a colored relief of a stag. He turned the vase around and, by moving his eye up to a glass lozenge on the opposite side, he could see the same picture of the stag much reduced in size, like looking through the opposite end of a telescope.

There was yet another room, farther on, beyond the dining hall. Its great dimness could be glimpsed through a half-open door. He put the crystal vase back in the dresser and stood for a while listening.

Then, without making a noise, he entered the blue room.

He left much later, as silently as he had entered, crossed the house once more, and went down to the courtyard. There was a tree at the far end that produced small black berries: they could be fired with a peashooter and someone reckoned they were poisonous. Digging about there one afternoon, he had felt something hard and heavy. When he brushed off the soil and cleaned it with sandpaper, he discovered it was a lead bullet. Then he remembered that once, where the courtyard stood, there had been a munitions dump. But he didn't know when. The person who had told him wasn't exactly sure; he too had been told about it, didn't know whether it was during World War I or perhaps even in Napoleonic times.

He wandered between two patches of garden which, though bare and flowerless, were edged by a black spongy residue, coal slag that sometimes formed in the boiler. In one corner of the courtyard there was a strange broad tangled mass. It was hard to say whether it was a piece of hedge that had grown too large and had come to resemble a tree, or a tree that looked like a hedge. Whatever it was, one day a hawk had gone to perch in the maze of its branches, at least so they said, and each time he went past he peered in among the thin intricate foliage, frightened of seeing the dark, still shadow of the bird of prey.

On the other side of the courtyard, by a longer patch of soil, the flat, wide tip of a large stone emerged barely visible from the ground. More than once he had tried to get it out but, digging around it, he realized it had to be enormous. Even some builders who were in the courtyard had tried one day without success. So he had reached the conclusion that this was the summit of a marble mountain buried underground which held the whole courtyard raised in the air. Walking around the garden, he sometimes passed over it, stopped for a moment, closed his eyes, and thought: "There, I'm now on the summit!" He swayed, felt dizzy, had to suddenly open his eyes again so as not to fall.

Before going back up into the house, he pulled open the heavy garage door, unscrewed the tank of the automobile, and sniffed the gasoline until he felt almost faint. Then he climbed the kitchen steps, walked along the corridor, through the anteroom, into the dining hall.

From there he moved silently, almost on tiptoe, into the blue room.

It was dark inside, as the windows were nearly always shut and an old dark blue wallpaper, slightly torn here and there, covered all the walls.

A blind old lady lived there. Everyone in the house called her "the Signorina."

He approached her bed in silence, gazed at her wide-open eyes that looked like globes of plastic, caught her murmuring a prayer. Her hair, very long, thick, and jet-black despite her age, flowing inexplicably from that small bony head, formed an intricate mass on the pillow. The Signorina turned two or three times in the bed, murmured something else, then went back to sleep with her hands together on the fold of the sheet. He often stared at those hands: they were long and light, almost weightless. Arthritis had produced two lumps, one on the wrist and the other on the last bones of the fingers, deforming them. They looked like the stylized image of a wing in flight.

Before supper the Signorina got out of bed and shuffled to the kitchen. When she returned to the blue room, her hands feeling for the doors, he ran noiselessly beside her, passing with her through the empty rooms, the anteroom, the dining hall, which had a small revolving hatch in one wall, once used to serve dishes without any need to enter the hall. When he was very small, he could get inside that rotating mechanism and was able in that way to move from one room to the other, or whirled around inside it, propelled by unknown hands which stopped the carousel only after he had shouted out and banged his little fists inside the wooden cylinder.

He waited for the Signorina to get back in bed, then sat

in a corner with schoolbooks on his knees. In a small circle
of light he tried to calculate the volumes of solids, polyhedra
with their many opened-out sides, planes that cut or intersected pyramids and cylinders at an angle, the right-angle
triangle shown turning around one of its legs to form a cone.

It was in that same point of the room, one day, while the
Signorina was trying hard to find something in a cupboard,
that he made an incredible discovery: he had dropped his
underpants to inspect his genitals when he noticed an infinity of black dots had appeared all around.

For several days he said nothing to anyone. When he
wasn't in the blue room he shut himself in the cellar, beneath
the great stairway. He entered through the concealed doorway, painted to look like the panels on the wall of the stairway
with a wide wainscot below, went down without switching
on the light, down a worn and uneven flight of steps, and
when he was down in the large underground room, he threw
himself onto the woodpile, two tall orderly stacks that gradually diminished over the winter, or onto the last remaining heap of coal, because they had recently replaced the coal
furnace with one that burned oil and, in that position, barely
illuminated by the scant light that came in from the window
grating, he uncovered his genitals, staring at them without
daring to touch them, as his heart beat so fast that it seemed
to suffocate him.

Or he would climb the wooden steps that led from
the kitchen to a small study and from here, pulling open a

heavy door, climbed a rusty iron ladder that reached up to the roofs with their grimy skylights dotted here and there and, higher still, to a terrace where he could lie on the paving and gaze at the sky through numerous strands of rusty wire on which the thin extremities of creepers had once twisted and clung, of which nothing now remained apart from a few black, almost carbonized remains and small isolated gnarls. Turning to one side he could look down, through the hole of a water gutter, to the courtyard and the back of a clinic and, a little farther on, in the street, the trucks that regularly transported milk to the nearby dairy in long sealed tanks, with small metal ladders for the men who had to climb up to their great metal mouths.

As the days passed, the black spots became even denser and soon an enormous quantity of small dark hairs had completely changed the appearance of his genitals. "What will happen now?" he wondered. What terrible illness had he picked up? What was he turning into?

He spent more time than usual hidden away in the blue room, unbeknown to the Signorina. Only the tortoise, which moved silently around the house, betrayed his presence now and then with a small noise. He moved about and found it motionless in some corner of the room, with part of its face out of its shell, watching him intently as he examined his genitals in the small circle of light from the lamp over the headboard of the bed.

The cat, on the other hand, hadn't been seen for some

while in the blue room, ever since its feces had been found in one corner of the room. It had been grabbed that day by the neck and its nose thrust into the feces, time and again, despite its furious snarls and great swirling of claws in all directions. For several days the feces had remained plastered onto the skin of its nose and left to dry so that it wouldn't forget.

Two guinea pigs that had wandered the house at some previous time, scattering droppings over the floor, were already dead. One of them, left out in the courtyard for a whole night, was found frozen, flat out on the first step up to the kitchen, while the other had died for the opposite reason in the furnace room. It had been shut up there at night for quite some while, where it had taken to warming itself by sticking its nose into a fairly wide space between two sections of the furnace. One morning it was found dead in that position. For several days he checked out the space by sticking the palm of his hand very low down, at the point where the guinea pig would push in its little nose, and it seemed impossible to him that such a gentle heat could have slowly cooked its brain, especially at night.

While conducting these experiments, he happened to move his hips close to the furnace and the heat stirred a sensation he had never felt before. And so he dropped his pants and pushed his penis, slightly swollen, into the gap higher up. It fitted perfectly inside and he hardly even noticed that its inner walls at that point were very hot and almost scorching. He realized after a while, all at once, felt an acute pain, like a burning at the tip of his penis which in the meantime had swollen even more, and had a job to get it out of the scalding gap. When the pain had become unbearable he pulled his hips back with a jolt. For a moment he could feel a resistance from the tip of his enlarged penis, trapped in the tight crack, pressed like putty against its inside walls. Next moment, he was on the ground. He peered at the furnace, sure that he would see his torn and bleeding penis still trapped in the crevice.

But there was nothing there: his penis was still dangling between his legs, no sign of blood, only larger, red, distended, and he reckoned this was what those of adults must look like.

Sometimes, during his long visits to the blue room, he could hear insistent rhythmic noises from the house next door, muffled by the thick walls. So far as he knew, beyond the blue room was the bedroom of another house where a sportsman lived.

Sometimes, after the noises had stopped, he broke the silence, stamped his feet on the floor, pretending he was coming into the room only then, greeted the Signorina, and sat down by her bed. After a while he would run to the kitchen, quietly take a teaspoonful of ground coffee and, trying not to spill it along the way, would carry it quickly to the Signorina, who adored it. He remembered in these moments how he had once heard that the berries in the courtyard were poisonous and had taken one and squashed it between his fingers onto a heaped spoon of ground coffee. The small drop of blackish liquid was absorbed straightaway by the dry powder. He had given the teaspoon to the Signorina, who had quickly sucked the contents. He watched her with his eyes fixed, imagining she would suddenly let out a cry, would put her hands to her throat and open her mouth, panting for breath. But time passed and the Signorina carried on quietly sucking the ground coffee, which slowly dissolved in the middle of her tongue, not even noticing the strange flavor that had penetrated it.

He would remain in the room till night came. Generally speaking, if he wasn't asleep by the kitchen stove with his face not far from its red-hot rings, or wandering around the courtyard or in the cellar or on the roof terrace, then he would be lying silently in one corner of the blue room on an old couch with dark blue threadbare cushions.

Before going to bed he'd find a book by rummaging the drawers, some of which he could hardly open as they were so full of tangled string, scraps of paper, and bundles of photographs. He read under the blankets for hours. One of the people in the house would often burst into his room unannounced, late at night, tell him to switch off the light, say terrible things would happen to him. But there again he already knew: he would get sick and then die mad. All the more since now there was a new, inescapable reason. He turned the light off for ten minutes or so, then switched it back on.

He carried on reading, curled up, ready to turn the light back off and hide the book under the blankets if anyone returned to check, holding the edge of the pages so as not to make a noise. Maybe this was why he so often cut his fingers: they were painful cuts, razor-thin and bloodless.

Some time earlier he had found a place to put the books he was gradually discovering, forgotten in drawers. He lined them along a shelf on the wall above the couch in the blue room. Along with the books, an Italian dictionary, and several newspapers raked up around the house, he also kept a comb there, and the bullets he had found in the courtyard. In fact, after the first bullet, he had found some more while digging under the low wall separating the courtyard from the back of the clinic, where he had found a whole mass of them. He only had to scratch with his fingernails to see a bullet immediately appear, and it was a great thrill to handle that solid, heavy object, hidden in the ground until just a second before.

He cleaned and polished the bullets with sandpaper, then packed them into a glass jar from which he had removed the jam label. The jar grew slowly heavier and sometimes, while the Signorina was asleep, he couldn't resist the temptation of shaking it to hear the dull sound of the bullets as they rattled against each other.

As he was digging under the wall, a man rode around one of the patches of garden for a whole hour, on a scooter he had just purchased. He must have decided to do the whole running-in around the courtyard. He passed in front of the hawk's hedge, then jolted over the slight up-and-down of the rock. The boy meanwhile imagined that sooner or later the man would fall off, and that if he fell at that point, the rock would smash the whole scooter.

One day, while he was on the couch holding a book of poems, the Signorina got out of bed to urinate. She lifted the lid of the commode and, before sitting down, pulled up her night-dress, revealing for an instant her skinny thighs and a small tuft of hairs that were thin but as black as those on her head. The scene lasted only a moment but, for the first time, he didn't look away. As the Signorina urinated he remained fixed where he was, holding his breath. From the commode came the sound of the urine that streamed down into the already half-filled basin. Once again, at the end, the Signorina pulled up her nightdress twisted around her thighs, revealing for an instant a bloated stomach, misshapen by a hernia. Just as she was standing up, he saw something glint from under the tuft of hairs and, before realizing it was in fact a drop of urine on the point of falling, he thought he had glimpsed some tiny metallic object protruding slightly from her abdomen. The Signorina lowered her nightdress, sat down on the bed, and still, as she lifted her legs and her deformed feet to slip them under the sheets, his eyes remained fixed, trying, in the only available moment, to cast his eyes deep between the bony legs beneath her nightdress. But he could see nothing. Only when the Signorina had pulled the blankets up to her chin did he turn his head, which felt rigid, to make sure no one had entered the room in the meantime, that no one was standing motionless in the doorway, that the tortoise wasn't hiding under a piece of furniture spying on him, waiting for the right moment to emerge silently from its hiding place and, after a frantic half-day journey through the rooms, to reach the kitchen and announce to everyone what incredible business was going on in the blue room.

But no one came in. Silently he got up from the couch, went through the dining hall, his own room, the anteroom, slowly opened the door to the stairway, and ran skipping down the low, wide steps. He went down into the cellar, threw himself onto a pile of coal under the grating, and remained there for an immeasurable time. There was a smell of wood and coal. From the farthest corners and from the alcoves came sounds of small animals nesting in secret parts of the fuel stacks. The lumps of coal under his back didn't hurt but were soft and welcoming and gradually molded themselves perfectly to his shape. Every now and then he looked up at the grating, which was almost against the ceiling, and had a side view of the face of someone passing on the sidewalk in front of the house.

Time passed and even the dim light that entered through the grating was fading little by little. As evening came, the cellar grew gradually darker, black as the heap of coal on which he lay.

He remained quite still for a long while, then left the cellar, groping his way with both hands along the two walls of stacked wood, careful not to trip over the dry twigs that had come loose from the bundles and become buried in the sawdust. He went into the furnace room next to the cellar. To reach it he had to pass through a storeroom filled with sacks of rice and flour, the floor entirely covered with potatoes. He reached the oil-fired furnace, aflame once more and full of color, which seemed vast in that small room with its compressed roar. That very same place, until a few months ago, had housed a rather smaller black coal furnace with masses of clocks and dials. When anyone in the house had gone down to refill it, he went along to watch. If he peered in through the opening, the red heat would immediately scorch his face while the coal was being shoveled in. Sometimes inside the furnace there was a buildup of clinker, material that would no longer burn, that formed in the grate. He would put a long pair of tongs into the mouth of the furnace and pull it out in white-hot lumps. He would wait for them to turn black and cool, like carbonized sponges, then carry them into the yard and lay them with the others that edged the patches of garden.

Before installing the new oil-fired furnace, several men dug a great hole in one part of the yard, dropping an enormous black, tar-covered tank into it. They had brought it in many separate pieces and welded it together in position. When it was still not completely closed, he climbed inside, one evening at dark, trembling. Once welded and tarred, the furnace was left for several days in the middle of the yard, close to the hawk's hedge, looking like a submarine ready to submerge.

He placed a hand on the furnace, which at that very moment had gone off. So he turned the lever on the thermostat to maximum and the burner suddenly reignited with a roar, as though it were about to explode and destroy the house. And from a slight glow he could see that a great flame had suddenly erupted inside.

Once out of the room, he was soon back upstairs in the house. Passing the coatrack, he brushed his hand against the opossum collar, then went to look at the sword hidden in one of the bedrooms. He unsheathed it and tried to swing it in the air. But it was heavy and he could hardly move it. He took the hunting horn from the wall and began blowing it through pursed lips, thinking he would give it all he had. He could feel his head fill with blood in the enormous effort and it seemed to swell like a balloon, but, at the very moment he feared it would explode, the mouth of the horn gave out an almighty blast, which, after traveling the interminable spiral, erupted into the house, prompting cries of alarm in even the farthest rooms.

A man arrived the next day from the countryside. He had a small motorcar from which one of the front seats would usually be removed to allow more space. The floor was always covered with several inches of soil so that corn seeds dropped from sacks during transport would take root and quickly grow and, as the man didn't sweep them away, they soon formed a bristling carpet of green plants by the driver's seat, flattened and spoiled here and there by the weight of the sacks.

That day the man unloaded a sack of rice, one of fish, and a live pheasant. He carried the sack of fish to the bathroom and, before opening it to tip it into the bathtub full of water, rested it for a moment on the floor. The sack moved about, shaking from one side to another, jolted by the fish wriggling inside.

Meanwhile, the pheasant was left loose in the house. Before being sacrificed it could wander calmly for days and days along the corridor, into the anteroom, into the other rooms with their vaulted or coffered ceilings, and even, with a little luck, along the stairway, with its golden feathers.

The same had happened the previous year to a turkey, which would sometimes appear even in the blue room with its ugly neck full of wattles and droplets of flesh. It was immense, and if it had attacked him, he thought, he wouldn't have managed to protect himself. But after a few days two helpers had brought it to the ground and chopped its head off with a single blow.

Two builders arrived in the clinic courtyard and started working in one corner. He climbed into the tree with the black berries to get a better view, positioning himself in the middle of a large fork. But not even from there could he understand what they were doing. So he climbed down and returned to digging in search of bullets, which had now almost completely filled the glass jar on the shelf. He went back up into the house. In the corridor, he leapt up to grab one of the iron bars, doing several twirls and pull-ups.

During those days there was much coming and going and the only conversation was about documents and lawyers as proceedings were going on against the nuns of the next-door clinic. The people in the house were claiming to have rights over several square yards of the clinic courtyard. They wanted to use that pocket of land to extend the kitchen and build a new balcony above. He was therefore always worried about meeting people in the study or in the anteroom and, since he could no longer climb into the serving hatch and pass unnoticed into the dining hall, he had to take a much longer route to reach the blue room, where no one ever went.

One weekend morning, while he was combing his hair in a piece of mirror propped on the shelf, the Signorina got up from the bed to urinate. He turned inadvertently, waiting for the moment when she would pull up her nightdress. As she approached the commode, the Signorina once again bared her legs and the lower part of her pubic hair, while he, though frightened at the idea someone might arrive that very moment, couldn't stop himself moving a few steps toward the commode to take a closer look. He stayed standing in the middle of the room, a few yards from the Signorina, who meanwhile had carefully sat down. Having urinated, she got up to return to her bed and, despite the proximity, he managed to see even less than the day before. Her sex, glimpsed once again for just a second, seemed something shapeless, indefinable. No opening could be seen beneath that thin covering of hairs that ended in a moist, dripping point: there was no way of understanding where the urine came out.

He went back to sit on the couch, looking once again at the door to check no one had entered in the meantime. Then he lay down, while his breathing settled. Beneath the large painted head of the tearful Mary Magdalene over her bed, the small bony head of the Signorina rested on the pillow and was muttering a prayer in Latin, in the singsong cadence of a nursery rhyme. Stretched out on the couch, he was wondering why he hadn't obtained a clearer view of the Signorina's sex, to understand once and for all exactly how it was made. Was it due maybe to the general darkness in the room? Or the wrong angle? Or the Signorina's virginity? Perhaps her sex had slowly closed up, like with certain gastropods. How could his eyes overcome that subtle yet impenetrable barrier?

Then he remembered there used to be a torch in the drawer of the kitchen table. He hurried to check. Yes, it was still there. While he was quietly slipping it into his pocket, they asked him to go fetch a basket of potatoes from the storeroom.

He went down to the cellar. It took him some time to shoo off the pheasant in the anteroom that wanted to get through the open door and down the stairway.

In the storeroom, having filled the basket, he tidied up the potatoes that were still there. They had begun to sprout as they lay heaped on the floor, so he pulled the shoots off with his hand. He stayed there for a while, listening to the tapping of a typewriter and several voices coming from an office next to the storeroom.

Later he went down to the yard to dig. It was now most unlikely the Signorina would sit on the commode again that day.

A couple of hours later he went back up to the house with another twenty bullets. He had never found so many at one time! He had to cup both hands together to carry them. In the kitchen he asked for a new sheet of sandpaper, some detergent, and a piece of rag. But there was no rag. Finally, rummaging through a pile of laundry, he found a pair of child's underpants ruined by a large burn mark the shape of a flatiron. It must have been left on them by mistake while it was hot, and they were now beyond use.

Before supper he put the clean and polished bullets into the glass jar, which was already nearly full, and also found a place for the torch on the shelf.

But he had to wait until the next day to catch the Signorina once again as she got up to urinate. He wasn't in the blue room but had gone out for a moment when some sounds, which couldn't have been those of the athlete's equipment on the other side of the wall, made him hurry back. But perhaps it was too late, perhaps he had missed the only moment when he could have pointed the torch. The Signorina, however, had only just got out of bed. Standing a few yards away, he shone the torch, pointing it at the very moment when the Signorina was pulling up her nightdress. But the tiny beam of light, illuminating the pubic hair for an instant, made it even more opaque and impenetrable. At that very moment he heard a slight noise behind him. He turned at once toward the door, in panic: it was the pheasant, strutting into the room, tapping its claws on the wooden floor.

The torch slipped out of his hand and fell with a clatter.

"Who is it? Who is it?" the Signorina asked anxiously, before getting back in bed without urinating.

Her small head was slightly raised by the pillow and she was peering intently at the room with her plastic globes.

"Who is it?" she asked again, more loudly.

Then, with a slight groan, she turned to one side, shaking her legs several times as if in a gesture of anger and despair.

The pheasant, frightened by the falling torch, had run off. It could be heard scampering away, its claws must have been moving with difficulty, sliding on the polished floor of the dining hall. He picked up the torch and left the room, not making a sound. He went down to the cellar and on the heap of coal he wondered whether, even without seeing it, the Signorina could have been aware of that tiny beam of light on her body. To try and find out, he stripped naked from the waist down, shut his eyes and when he seemed unable to see anything, not even the small blotches and colored dots wandering across his retina, he pointed the torch against his genitals, switching it on and off several times. But he seemed to notice each change, as if the light, penetrating his flesh, was making it swell. How could it be? Perhaps, he thought, this happened because he knew beforehand. Perhaps, having to operate the torch, and keeping his eyes tightly closed at the same time so as not to see, put him into a state of overexcitement and prevented him from relaxing and being objective.

Later, when it was evening outside and the whole cellar had become as dark as the heap of coal on which he lay, he tried once again to flash the light on and off his genitals. His eyes were now accustomed to the darkness, it was enough for him to gently close them so as not to see the slightest reflection of the tiny beam of light. All of a sudden he felt his body grow rigid. He had to turn stomach down, onto the heap of coal, and after an interminable period during which he lost all self-control, he sat up again and tried to look: the coal was splattered with whitish blotches he had never seen before that could only have come out of some part of his body as a result of an internal laceration. He started crying, thinking he was really going to die.

In the light he saw that dust and tiny slivers of coal had become glued to his body and that his penis, where it wasn't plastered with coal, was red and distended like the day when it had been trapped in the gap between two segments of the furnace.

He lay on the coal heap for quite some time and, seeing that nothing was happening, he thought it must be a very slow death, something resembling a very long bleeding or draining of liquid. He decided to get up and, with a piece of coal, he managed to cover over the fragments of whitish matter, which were now somewhat smaller, perhaps absorbed by the coal, and had become more transparent. He left the cellar, removed the traces of coal from his clothing as best he could before going back into the house, pretending to have come from outside.

Over the next few days he rarely went into the blue room. From the terrace he spent hours watching the builders working in the clinic yard. They were building something strange: it looked like a miniature house. But he couldn't work out what it was for. Might it have something to do with theater? Perhaps they wanted to put on puppet shows to amuse young patients. This was why they had built this thing, like a small fixed outdoor stage. But, in that case, why build it on the ground? Was it some strange cage for keeping small animals, like guinea pigs or white mice for example? Perhaps it was a miniature shrine, built to let patients attend Mass in the yard during the hottest months. But it seemed too large for a shrine, and they'd have built it at least a few feet from the ground.

The trucks still went by at regular intervals with their stainless steel tanks full of milk and sometimes they looked exactly like those that carried gasoline or other inflammable material, with the only difference that they had no warning sign on the back.

The few times he entered the blue room, he let the Signorina hear him straightaway and went to sit by her bed. Since he often wrote poems during that period, he would sometimes read one to her.

"That's lovely!" the Signorina remarked at the end of the reading.

"But I don't like it!" he complained.

Then he blew the edge of the sheet in his hand, producing a sound like that of paper being torn, while the Signorina despaired and held her hand out to try to stop him.

One day he took some books from the shelf and read these lines to the Signorina, making her think they were his own work:

At this he said, they each took the two-handled cup
and having made a libation, followed Odysseus back
    to the ships.
Patroclus then commanded his men and maidservants
to make a soft bed for Phoenix without delay;
they obeyed, laid out the bed as he wished,
fleeces, a blanket, soft linen sheets.

And the old man lay there and awaited the holy dawn.
Achilles slept at the far end of the sturdy tent,
and beside him a woman he had taken from Lesbos,
the daughter of Phorbas, fair-cheeked Diomede;
Patroclus lay on the other side, and with him
shapely Iphis, whom noble Achilles had given to him
when he captured rocky Skyros, the fortress of
    Enyeus.

"How beautiful!" the Signorina exclaimed at the end.

He immediately pretended to tear up the paper, while her hands floundered in the void.

"Do you want me to read you another?" he asked.

"Yes, but don't destroy it afterward!" the Signorina pleaded.

He began to read once more:

While the king rests
on his couch,
my lavender releases
its gentle fragrance.
My beloved for me is
like a sachet of myrrh
that rests between my breasts.
My beloved for me is
like a cluster of henna
that blossoms in the vineyards of Engedi.

At the end of the reading he pretended once again to tear up the paper. The Signorina pleaded desperately, with her head on the pillow and her hands twisted.

He pretended to leave the room, but instead went and lay on the couch, continuing to read in silence:

> Ah! my child, why did I, your wretched mother, rear
> you?
> If only you had remained with your ships, without
> tears
> Without grief, since your fate is short, not long!
> Now you are doomed to swift and painful death
> It was by ill fate that I bore you in our house.

Meanwhile, he followed the passing of time in the reflection of a tiny cone of light that entered from a crack between the shutters and gradually faded, darkening against the vault of the ceiling. After a while the Signorina, thinking she was alone, got up to urinate. He continued to watch her, not moving from the couch, but, perhaps because of some greater circumspection on her part, he could see absolutely nothing, not even the end part of her tuft of hairs.

Much later, as the Signorina seemed to be drowsing, almost entirely hidden beneath the blankets, he stamped his feet on the floor pretending to return to the room. He went to sit by her bed, resting his head on the fold of the sheet. Then he took one of her hands, rested it on his hair, and said:

"Feel how long it is!" "Oh, oh . . ." the Signorina repeated several times, as her hand moved down to feel for the ends of his hair. And even after she had found them she continued stroking his hair lightly with her hand, which resembled a wing in flight, and he couldn't remember anyone ever having caressed him like that.

The Signorina wasn't born blind, she went blind just before thirty. The strange thing was that after thirty more years of total blindness, for some reason the doctors couldn't understand, her sight returned for a few months.

It had happened early one spring. In semidarkness she had managed, after so long a time, to distinguish the shapes of faces and even of printed words. Over those months, day by day, she had managed to read the whole of Manzoni's *The Betrothed*. Then the semidarkness thickened once again and, for ten years since, there had been no further repetition.

People used to come to consult the Signorina in two particular circumstances: for predictions on the weather and for finding some lost object. But her help came in useful on a whole series of other cases: to assure the prompt arrival of a letter, to learn what was inside a package that had to remain sealed, to know what time the alarm clock had stopped, to find out about water leaks even before they could be seen on ceilings.

During those days he had asked her about the miniature house being built in the yard of the clinic. What could it be?

The Signorina shook her head and turned away as if to fall asleep. But he reckoned she was really only pretending and for some unknown reason she didn't want to tell him something that she had guessed perfectly well.

Meanwhile, work continued in the clinic yard. The brick walls of the tiny house were plastered and colored yellow, an iron door was fixed to it, and sticking out of the roof was a fine chimney, long and straight, with a small cone-shaped cap on the top. The door, of course, meant it couldn't be a puppet theater, just as the chimney excluded the possibility of it being a shrine.

Once the works were complete, the little house looked fine against the corner of the perimeter wall, no longer with builders' equipment strewn about or overalls hung from the chimney like a coatrack. A small plinth at the base was painted darker and now other people in the house were starting to make all kinds of conjectures.

The Signorina's wooden commode was replaced by another, of aluminum, which also had wheels and could be pushed about the house. The wooden one, after so many years, had now become saturated with the smell of urine, and the Signorina's worsening health prevented her from walking about. And so at lunch time she sat on the closed lid of the new commode and was pushed through the rooms as far as the kitchen.

The pheasant still wandered the house. The day set for its sacrifice had passed, but the date had been postponed more than once because of its beauty and the pleasure of admiring it and allowing it to be admired as it strutted about the rooms and on the stairway.

As for the boy, he had started to fill a second jar with bullets and, after several days of experimentation, had managed to make some kind of ink from the black berries that grew on the tree in the yard. Having collected several cupfuls, he crushed the ripest in the garage. The biggest problem was how much water to add. With no water, the liquid was too gluey and didn't flow in the fountain pen, but if too much was added it became too faint and the letters were hard to make out.

At last he found the right mixture. With his fountain pen completely full and a good reserve supply in an ink pot, he could begin to study the possible ways of using it. After much thought, he decided to copy out passages from the books he kept on the shelf. He wrote them down on strips of paper of varying lengths, which he would then hide. Finding a hidey-hole wasn't easy. He checked out many places, but each had some drawback.

One day, as he was climbing the stairway into the house, he was surprised to notice the plaster head at the top of the banister rail. He didn't know who it was. He had once asked and been told it might be a poet, Giuseppe Parini, though perhaps it wasn't.

He stopped and put his hand on the plaster head. He tried moving it: it wasn't heavy. Then, on tipping it to one side, he discovered a hole at the center of the base. The head was hollow when he tapped it with his knuckles, so it must be empty inside. What better hiding place could there be! He could roll up strips of paper and slip them in. Once inside, they would flatten as they uncoiled, with no chance of coming out again. No one would ever find them.

As well as copying out passages, he started using the ink to write the diary that follows.

2

Today I found out what the miniature house is for.

I'd noticed a great commotion since early in the morning. Some nurses, nuns dressed in white, were going back and forth to the little house, opening and closing the door, kneeling down and looking inside, while a man in overalls was waving his hands as he tried to explain something.

After lunch I climbed up to the fork in the tree with the black berries and could see smoke coming out of its chimney, which wafted out as it hit the cement cap at the top. But there was nobody around the little house. Gradually, as time went by, there was an increasingly strange smell, sweetish but at the same time pungent, which irritated the nose and throat. Maybe, I thought, they want to raise the temperature by a few degrees to protect the plants in the surrounding flowerbeds.

I climbed down from the tree and started digging. I found a few bullets, nine, and went back up into the house. There too they had seen the smoke from the chimney of the little house and noticed a strange smell in the air.

In the small study above the kitchen I took some binoculars from a drawer and climbed onto the roof terrace. I lay flat on my stomach and pointed the binoculars out of the hole in the gutter. After ten minutes or so, since there was nothing to see, I got up to return to the house. But at that very moment I saw some white shadows behind the windows of the clinic. I dropped back down on my stomach with binoculars at the ready. Two nuns came out. After looking around for a moment, they crossed the yard to the little house. They were holding things with both hands, in such a way as to hide them with their bodies. In front of the little house, they crouched to the ground and put those things down: two shiny stainless steel basins. Though they were trying to hide them with their clothes, at the moment when they lifted the basins to throw the contents into the little house through its open door, I saw for a few instants that they were full of red things that moved about as though they were rubber. Reddish and gray lumps slid out and there were also long slimy things among them that looked like snakes. Finally, since something must still have been in there, they shook the basins two or three times and something very large flew out, bluish gray in color, followed by something liquid.

I was flabbergasted. Though I was sure they couldn't see me, I let the binoculars drop to the ground and rolled away from the hole, keeping flat on my back, lying on the terrace. I still couldn't understand what I had seen. They were certainly things pulled out from deep invisible places, long things, lumps, dead snakes that left a wet trail and floated in blood.

I went down to the kitchen to tell them. Two went off to the clinic. They returned after an hour and reported what had happened: the nuns had tried at first to deny it, but then, when faced with the evidence, had admitted it was in fact an oven. Twice a week they will be burning bits removed during operations: tumors, polyps, amputated limbs, gauze covered with blood and puss and other things.

The clinic oven is all they talk about in the house. They have ordered the nuns to knock it down. Otherwise they'll take legal action.

I've made a discovery. For several days I've been hearing strange noises in my room. At first I thought nothing of it. I thought the athlete on the other side of the blue room wall must have started using some new, noisier equipment. Or that someone was working against the vault of the arch in the entrance hall, right beneath my room. The only thing that surprised me was that the noise could also be heard at night.

Today, as the noise had become even more insistent, I checked my room all over, opened the drawers and looked under the furniture and behind the pictures. But I haven't found anything that might explain those noises. I stopped searching, pretending not to notice them. After an hour I thought I had found the place where the noises were coming from. Under a desk, a few inches from the floor, there's a tin drawer that goes inside the wall. At one time, before they installed the central heating system, in its place was a chimney pipe connected to a stove. The drawer is there now to close off the long shaft that runs inside the wall and up to a large skylight on the roof.

I went to the drawer and, by pulling it, managed to remove it from the wall. There was a dead bird inside, half buried under some soot, dust, and plaster. I took the drawer into the kitchen and tipped the bird and everything else in the bin. Before pushing the drawer back into the wall I wanted to have a look inside the hole. I bent down and looked inside but it was all black and I couldn't see a thing. I went into the blue room and got the torch down from the shelf. Back in my room, I bent down and aimed the beam of light into the hole. There was another bird inside, standing, motionless, petrified. It was facing one side, and its little eye, caught in the light, staring at me, seemed to be made of colored glass. Even though I kept the torch shining against its small body, it remained so still that I couldn't figure whether it was alive or had been dead for some time. I tried flashing the light on and off several times. It didn't move. Then, even though I was afraid, I stretched my hand into the hole to catch it. At that very instant the little bird shot out of the darkness. It seemed terrified, flapped its wings against the walls and crashed several times into the furniture. It remained stunned for a few moments, then suddenly leapt up and began flying around the room again. It was like one of those little automobiles that never stop moving, even when they bump into walls or the legs of furniture, and their tiny engine roars even louder, swerves a little to one side and races on again, searching for other routes.

I rushed to open a window. The little bird sped across the room and launched itself into the void. Outside, it soared up and down in the air two or three times, falling headlong, plunging vertically, and each time seemed on the point of crashing to the ground. Then, in spite of its days spent inside the drawer, hungry, stuck next to the other little bird already dead, it darted up high and in a few seconds, fluttering its wings that seemed electric, it became an almost invisible dot in space, and I couldn't figure how those tiny wings could carry it so far and so quickly into the sky, where only hawks generally fly.

I went and told the Signorina all about it. And as I carried on with my story she gradually lifted her head, straightening herself until she was sitting in the bed with her hands bent, and in the end burst into the most thunderous laughter I had ever heard in the house.

I went down into the courtyard to dig and found twelve bullets. I cleaned them and, before going to put them in the jar, I hung on the iron bar in the corridor. I did ten twirls and two pull-ups.

Just now I copied a passage onto a strip of paper. I felt my heart pounding as I wrote it out. I rolled it up and went to put it inside Parini. As I expected, once inside the cavity of the head, the strip of paper uncoiled so that it was flat. I'll write the passage down here, as I will do each time from now on:

Oh, run away, my beloved,
like a gazelle
or a young stag
over the scented hills!

Yesterday I wrote nothing as I was sick. In the morning, before leaving home, I went to sit for a few minutes in the blue room without letting myself be heard. I was leaving the room when I realized that the tortoise, hidden under some furniture the same color as its shell, was looking at me without making the slightest noise. In the semidarkness of the blue room it was almost impossible to make it out.

I tiptoed toward it and lifted it very high. I made not a sound and the tortoise was incapable of crying out, so the Signorina, though she was awake nearby, could have known nothing about the furious battle that was going on a few yards away from her. The tortoise shrank completely into its shell. I left the room and, having hidden it inside my schoolbag, I walked through the whole house and down to the garage without the tortoise, closed inside, managing to attract anyone's attention by crying for help. I closed the garage door from inside and removed the tortoise, whose head was partly out of its shell trying to work out what was going on. I examined the various tins of paint lined up on a shelf and eventually chose one that had the same aluminum color I had used a few days ago to paint the stove pipe in the kitchen. I thought the metallic effect of the aluminum would be better than all the other colors in marking the presence of the tortoise in the blue room. I diluted the color with a little turpentine and painted the shell of the tortoise before taking it back into the house, pretending that I'd forgotten something.

In the afternoon, as·I was sitting silently in the blue room, the Signorina got up from the bed to go to the commode. I felt a great anger inside. I took the torch and tiptoed immediately to the center of the room, and while the Signorina was pulling up her nightdress I moved even closer. When I pointed the light I was hardly three feet away and, moving my head forward and looking so closely at those thin hairs that still revealed absolutely nothing, I moved the torch closer, almost touching her and, since everything seemed so frightening and terrible to me, for a moment I seemed on the point of reaching out and touching the Signorina in that place, or of falling to the ground, or of making her fall by knocking her with my face.

I hurried back to the couch and felt sick for some while. All at once I saw the tortoise in the room, standing motionless, perfectly disguised beneath the new commode, which is the same color as its painted shell, with its head almost completely shrunk inside. At that moment I understood what I had always thought about that tough little creature, namely that it must be infinitely cruel, malicious, and the fact that it can't show its cruelty didn't make it any less ferocious and deadly. But there again, is it true it cannot show it? Or does it not have its own ways, like everything else?

Perhaps it's enough for it, after long calculation, to slightly move the smallest and most insignificant of objects it finds around the house in order to trigger a chain reaction capable of bringing disaster.

I went up to the tortoise, which had withdrawn right into its shell. I picked it up and looked at it. It was now very old, no one knew exactly how old. They say they've always seen it around. During the war it had been left forgotten in the house while the others were evacuated to the countryside. When they came back, the whole house was badly damaged by the bombing, part of the vaulted ceiling in the entrance hall had collapsed and a beam had come down in another room, burying itself in the floor. There was plaster dust, shattered windows, rubble, and mold everywhere. And yet the tortoise emerged from a pile of bricks, splintered wood, and broken glass without betraying the slightest emotion and no one ever managed to explain how it had survived, how it had fed itself all that time.

The paint on the shell was now perfectly dry. I punched it twice but hurt my knuckles. Then I hurled it to the ground but couldn't break it. I gave it a kick, launching it as far as the dining hall. It passed between the table and chair legs and ended up hitting the false doorway at the far end. On hearing this noise, the Signorina began calling out:

"Who is it? Who is it?"

I left the blue room, went down to dig in the yard. There was the same smell in the air that I had sniffed two days ago.

This meant the nuns were using the oven more often than they had promised. I found five bullets in all. It looks as though the supply is running out. I'll have to dig somewhere else. I put the bullets in my pocket and, before going back up, went into the garage as I felt a great urge to get a smell of the gasoline. I opened the tank of the motor car and sniffed two or three times so deeply that I eventually felt an electric shock at the top of my nose, near to the brain. I dropped to the ground and passed out. I reckon I must have been on the floor ten minutes or so. I realized, as soon as I came round, that I had cut my lip as I fell. I was dazed, my cheek had been lying in a patch of oil that had seeped from the engine of the automobile. I went up to the kitchen and washed without letting anyone see me. I tried to stay for a while with my head by the stove to see if I felt any better.

At dinner I ate almost nothing. No one mentioned the tortoise. I went to bed early, not writing anything, not copying anything out, nor hanging on the bar in the corridor. In some of the bedrooms, wooden frames were bulging beneath the bedcovers, inside which were old cooking pans filled with ash and embers to warm the beds. They had only just been slipped in between the sheets and it looked as though large creatures had nestled there, hidden inside. In the bed with the sheepskin cover it seemed as if there was an enormous furry animal with its stomach in the air.

I got into bed and switched off the light without reading. I must have gone straight to sleep. Later, when they were all in bed, I was woken by a noise in the room. I lifted my head to listen more closely: it wasn't the usual sound that each different piece of furniture makes as it creaks in the dark. It was very close. The noise of the cat? Sometimes, when it is shut inside my room, it amuses itself by digging its claws into an old armchair behind the headboard of the bed. It has already damaged it in several places, ripping the leather to tiny shreds.

I switched the light on to look at the armchair: the cat wasn't there. I was afraid, so I got up to check around the room. There was no object or creature that could have caused noises like that, and all three doors were closed. I immediately thought of the little bird of the day before. I bent down under the desk and pulled the metal drawer out from the wall. But it was empty. I was afraid of sticking my hand into the hole without looking first with the torch since it might disturb something that had been there for goodness knows how long.

I made up my mind and put my hand inside, but there was nothing there, only a current of fresh air coming down from the roof. I went back to bed and when I heard those same noises a few minutes later, just a few inches from my head, I dived to the bottom of the bed like in a sack, expecting something enormous to descend on me at any moment. Then I must have fallen asleep.

Today I'm rather better. I did eight twirls on the bar in the corridor and two pull-ups. After several delays, they decided to kill the pheasant. I wasn't there when they did it, but it must have happened in the corridor because I heard voices and then some strange shrieking sounds coming from that direction early in the morning. It seemed like a person crying, but not like all the others. It was as though it had suddenly burst out crying without even having time to remember how to do it.

In the afternoon, the person cleaning the pheasant cut the whole end of her finger off with the poultry shears. Straightaway, instinctively, she went searching for it in the bin and in the drain hole, rummaging among the golden feathers, among the giblets that floated in the water, among the blood that was pouring from her finger like from a faucet, until she managed to find the missing end.

They took her to the emergency room of the clinic, where she was treated. But they didn't put the finger back on, they said they couldn't. She was away for a long time. From the bin I took the pheasant's longest and prettiest feathers, those golden tail feathers. I've decided to keep them. I've put them in the second jar of bullets, which is still half empty. They stick straight up on the shelf because I pushed their tips in among the bullets.

It is now evening. I'll finish writing and then go to bed. I won't do any copying out. I've just barred the door of the kitchen. Then I went down to fix the shutters to the door of the main stairway. I went to lie down for a while on the coal heap. It's called bituminous coal and I read in a book that it began to form in the late Paleozoic age. I went into the furnace room and turned the thermostat to maximum. The furnace suddenly burst into action and I thought it was about to explode.

A small dry crust has formed on my lip. It bothers me and each time, without thinking, I pull it off with my teeth.

I don't want to write today. I've found fourteen bullets. Maybe a new supply. I did eleven twirls and three pull-ups. Something has happened . . . but I'm not going to tell anyone. Toward evening I blew the hunting horn. I copied out four passages. Here they are:

"And why are you so certain?"

"To tell the truth, I don't know. I only know that I must win; that it is the only resource I have left. And perhaps this is why I feel I have to win every time."

Doctors Grant and Coldstream attended much to marine zoology, and I often accompanied the former to collect animals in tidal pools which I dissected as well as I could.

Cloning, however, consists of triggering the generative process starting from the nucleus of a body cell (for example of tongue, liver, intestines) and leaving the sexual cells out of play. Unlike these latter nuclei, those of the body (or somatic) cells contain the whole chromosome complement, forty-six in number. If this "yoke" is planted in the female egg previously deprived of its yoke (of only twenty-three chromosomes) the proliferation is set in motion as in natural fertilization, but with this difference: that the new individual does not result from the cross-fertilization of the chromosomes of two individuals of different sex (mother and father), but from the genetic information contained in the nucleus of the somatic cell of the donor. It is not a child of two parents, but of one single parent, so that the identity with this is absolute.

Charlotte gave him his place at Ottilie's side.

I didn't do much today. I learned a geometrical theorem. I didn't dig in the yard or hang on the bar. The oven smoked for a while: there'll also be a piece of finger inside. Before doing any writing I checked my hairs. They seem to keep on growing. And if they don't stop?

Just now I heard some shouts, but I couldn't work out which room they came from.

I slowly copied out a passage:

This is the exposition of the researches of Herodotus of Halicarnassus, in order that the actions of men may not be effaced by time, nor the great and wondrous deeds displayed both by Greeks and barbarians deprived of renown.

Before supper I looked out of one of the dining hall windows. I was careful not to lean too far so as not to fall onto the iron bar sticking out just below. It has a spike, like a lance, and at one time, on special occasions, they used to hang the flag on it.

A pack of hounds rushed out from an alleyway onto the sidewalk opposite. I was stunned, I'd never seen so many all together. I counted them: eighteen, each one different from the other. Some were thin, almost skeletal, while others were fat, with drooping stomachs, some were black and glossy, others yellowish or white, with dust and bits of light-colored stuff stuck to their fur. I thought maybe they had rolled just now on the floor of a carpenter's workshop down there in the alley, among wood shavings and heaps of sawdust. If it was carnival time, you might have thought of confetti or streamers left stuck to their backs. One in the middle had a leg missing, but trotted along just the same, keeping up with the others. Its paw had been cut right off and yet, with each step, perhaps out of habit, it moved the stump that poked out below its stomach.

People turned to watch them, moving to one side as they passed. All of a sudden I realized that behind, some distance away, two people, a man and a woman, were walking. I thought they might be the owners. But it was hard to tell:

they were too far back and at the same time too close for it to be thought they were there by chance.

Today I spied on the Signorina again. I went right up close with my face and pointed the torch. I was in danger of touching her at every tiny move she made. There was a strong odor and I felt an instinct to push her to the ground.

I paused to think for a while before writing this down. I don't know what word to use to describe what I experienced at that moment. I had to go to the dictionary. Having searched for some time, skipping from one word to another, I arrived at the word "instinct." The dictionary says: "instinct, a natural impulse that compels living creatures to perform certain acts useful for the preservation of existence." I don't know how all of this can be useful for the preservation of existence . . . I looked at another dictionary and found this other definition: "instinct, a series of innate, natural, hereditary, specific reactions responding to a particular necessity of life, therefore useful for the purposes of existence, even without the individual being conscious of such purposes."

So that's perhaps why I can't figure it out . . .

Now I'll put the dictionary away and carry on with the story. I couldn't see anything and was thinking up horrible things to say to the Signorina. I couldn't bear it any longer and wanted to bang her stomach with my head. When she sat down on the commode I thought: "Okay, enough!" I knelt on the ground in front of the commode, leaning on my elbows. I put my face down to the floor and turned to one side so as to look up. I was ready for anything: if someone had come in at that moment I'd have been finished. But I couldn't see into her body even like that.

I left the room thinking I would never go back in there again. I dug for a long while, reached close to the persimmon tree at the far end of the yard. Under it there are loads of bullets. Today alone, I found nineteen. I ran into the house to put them into the jar, forgetting that I had only just decided not to go back into the blue room under any circumstances. With more bullets, the pheasant feathers now stick up even straighter, they seem as if they are fixed in, and if I brush them with my hand they don't budge an inch.

Passing through the empty anteroom I saw the television had been left on, forgotten. I switched it off. The coat with the opossum collar was on the coatrack. I pulled it down and buried my face in its fur, soft as a cloud. My breath soon made it feel warm and my face, frozen after being out in the yard, began to get hot.

Today I didn't do any twirls, but I managed four pull-ups. I copied out these two passages:

Haud igitur dubiumst quin voces verbaque constent corporeis e principiis, ut laedere possint.

Lastly, traveling with advanced cholera is discouraged by all experts, it being recognized by experience in all places that the change of air develops the disease in individuals, and there being no shortage of examples of healthy people who on leaving an infected area have died of cholera on arriving in the arms of their family in a healthy area.

I'd have written nothing this evening, had it not been for something that happened which changed my mind. I had barred the kitchen door and closed the shutters on the stairway. Before going to bed I wandered around the rooms, not knowing what to do. Everyone else was still in the kitchen. When I left them they were arguing about the clinic oven, which smoked continually today for more than an hour, fouling the air. Someone went to complain to the nuns, who, on being told, said they would agree to limiting its use.

I went to a bedroom I hardly ever go into. It is full of wardrobes and chests of drawers, and on the floor there are always three pairs of felt slippers so as not to mark the wax-polished floor. Some time back I tried to slide across the room with them on my feet but I went too fast and ended up banging my head against the mirror. I almost smashed it.

It's a very big room. It also has three beds, two tables with four chairs each, and a fireplace they no longer use. In there they put piles of linen for which there's no space in the drawers: they wrap them in sheets of cellophane and put them in the mouth of the fireplace. These parcels are also on top of the wardrobes, almost as high as the wardrobes themselves, stacked up to the ceiling vault. In the room there is also a false doorway, always full of objects piled one on top of the other. You have to be careful when you open the door since, more often than not, everything rolls out. Once I quietly opened it and found several parcels, piled one on top of the other, neatly bound in wrapping paper. For a while I thought they might have been for me. Over the next few days I waited, but no present arrived and when I went back some time later to open the false door the colored packages were no longer there.

I had been looking around the room for a while when, all of a sudden, I had the feeling there was someone standing stock-still behind me, perhaps since I had entered. I felt a great chill around the top of my head. As I ran out of the room I turned back and saw there was a coatrack, jutting slightly from the wall, with three wooden spheres resembling a head and two short outstretched arms. Hanging from the highest sphere, goodness knows why, a bicycle wheel.

I'm sure it was the spokes of the wheel that had given me the idea of something there, of some kind of movement behind me. Maybe they had reflected some light, just for a second, from the mirror in front, and perhaps the mirror had in turn been struck by the reflection of headlights from some automobile passing along the road below the house that could perhaps have shone rays of light up against the window.

I went back to my room. Passing through the anteroom, I opened the door of the corridor: in the kitchen they were still talking. I rummaged through the drawers to look for a book. One drawer was so full that I couldn't open it. I pulled harder and, as it opened, an enormous pack of photographs that had been squashed flat, concertinaed up. A load of photos fell to the floor and I had to pick them up. But I couldn't get them back in the same drawer, so I put them into others too.

Back to writing. Something has happened . . . I was in bed for quite a while, still awake. I had already switched off the light and the house was completely silent. They had all gone to bed. I had heard them passing through the anteroom and through my room: I can now distinguish each of them from the different sound of their footsteps. Suddenly I heard a great bang. At first I thought war had broken out. I knew this was how it would happen, with no warning. A bomb must have hit the house, causing a piece of wall or a bed to fall against the door of my room leading to the anteroom. I switched on the light and lay quite still, covering my head with my arms. At any moment I would fall through the floor into the entrance hall and then, straight after, the whole house would collapse on top of me.

Nothing like this happened, but a few seconds later the door from my room to the anteroom was struck violently five times, louder and louder, probably with punches and kicks, but so violently that it seemed as though the wood was about to splinter. The whole door moved and shook, rattling forward with each blow as though its hinges were made of rubber.

I remained sitting on the bed for an eternity, but nothing else happened. When I next looked at the alarm clock, an hour had passed. Then I began to calm down. I got out of bed and checked the three doors of my room: they were all closed. I lifted a sack of rice which had been left forgotten in my room several days ago, and little by little I managed to push it up against the door to the anteroom. I waited for another while, even if time was now passing more quickly. All of a sudden I felt very calm and copied out a passage. What took place, after all, doesn't surprise me. I'm surprised only that it took so long to happen.

I shifted the sack of rice a little and went out into the anteroom. If someone was out there, all the better. But the anteroom seemed deserted, so far as I could guess, in the midst of all that darkness. I opened the door to the stairway and, amazed, I watched as my legs and arms passed through it. I slipped what I had written into Parini. On the floor was the stair carpet they put down for special occasions. I walked onto it and, without ever leaving it, began to go down the stairway. It wasn't difficult, despite the darkness, to follow the line of the carpet, which also stopped my feet from feeling the coldness of the marble. I reached the bottom, groped my way to the door, and went into the furnace room. I raised the thermostat to maximum and the furnace lit at once with its roar. The great flame that sprang up inside, filtering through a gap, cast a dim light over the whole room. I took the chair from behind the furnace. it is, in fact, an upholstered armchair, though the padding is starting to come out in various places. Not long ago it was in the house, then someone sat on it and broke a leg. So they carried it down. I sat on the chair, near the furnace, put my face right up to the point where the heat of the great flame filters out. Immediately I felt much better. My face began to scorch after a while. Time passed, and I remained sitting perfectly still and not even aware I was balancing on only three legs.

Now I'll go back to bed, even if it's almost morning and I don't think I'll sleep any more. I've moved the sack of rice: rather than leaving it upright I've laid it down in front of the door. Under the pillow I've hidden a knife I had brought to the room for cutting the pages of a book. I might even get some sleep.

I almost forgot to write down the last passage I've copied out:

In this area the sea went down to a depth of about 120–200 meters over which there loomed a sheer cliff, while the climate and vegetation were more the same as now, though slightly hotter. All of this data has been obtained from studying the fauna and species of leaves found (Salix, Castanea, Pinus, etc.). After the waters had receded (late Tertiary Period) there were four ice ages over the territory and the morainal ground over the clay is attributable to the last ice age.

There's havoc in the kitchen. I can hear shouting, everything is being smashed . . .

Two hours have gone by. I go back to writing. It was as if a wheel full of blades or metallic plates, the same for example as that of an electric razor but infinitely bigger, were leaping about in the kitchen, smashing everything, slicing through objects and wounding people, and nothing and no one could stop it, not even the objects being smashed to pieces and the cries of the people injured, roused increasingly by its own provocative capacity to make its victims suffer.

This evening I'm not doing any copying. I reckon I'll never do any more.

I'm going to resume writing after three months. I don't even know why. I may even continue over the coming evenings. But I'm not sure.

There's some sign of spring. The Signorina is getting worse. They now take food to her in bed. I've done some more digging and have almost filled a fourth jar with bullets. I read in the blue room, I've collected more books. The shelf is so full that there's no room for any more. I've taken to watching the television every now and then.

Last month they installed the telephone. It's my first opportunity to look at one close-up. They've put it on one of the walls in the anteroom, by the door to my room, and often when it rings I'm the first to answer. Sometimes I dial a number at random and listen to the voice that answers. I stand there in silence and try to imagine the shape of their face, what their hands are doing, what their house looks like, who lives there. I don't understand how sound waves go into such a small wire and then come out so far away. I've read that inside a telephone there's an electromagnet, a flexible disk, and carbon granules too.

The clinic oven is now lit almost every day. The nuns put the basins onto a trolley so that they can transport so much at once. It sometimes happens, as they push the cart over the gravel in the yard, that the wheels hit a stone a little larger than the others and something splashes out of the basins. The nuns then bend down to pick these bits up with their bare hands.

I've met a girl. For some time we've been going out in the afternoon on our bicycles. We go for a long ride, almost always the same. She has a curvature of the spine and she'll have to spend a long time wearing a heavy plaster cast that sticks out of her clothing as far as her chin. She has to keep her head bent back but still manages to steer her bicycle. She talks a lot and carries on talking even while she's pedaling, moving her large mouth, pointed toward the sky above the plaster cast.

Here many things have happened . . . I don't know if I can carry on writing. Everything is hanging by a thread.

3

Today I came across a diary I used to write years ago. They were sheets of paper, all rolled up together at the bottom of a drawer in my room, under a great mass of things. I pulled them out and began to read them. I had forgotten all about them and found it difficult at first to believe I had written them myself. They disturbed me. I can't explain why: now that they've reminded me about all that happened, I can say that so many things were missing from those accounts, details of far more importance. Indeed, the events that are described there are probably the most insignificant part of what happened over those days.

But why?

I found it difficult even to recognize the house that is described there. I've spent some time walking around the rooms and they seemed completely different from those of the diary. And yet every detail matches: the furniture, walls, and ceilings are exactly the same, and the stairway too, the iron bar in the corridor, the large bed with the sheepskin, the cellar, the blue room. And it is not just because, compared with the descriptions in the diary, the house now seems poorer and almost dilapidated in certain parts and at the same time richer and almost incredibly regal in others. It is not just because, even though it is very large, it no longer seems so grand, because it no longer seems so frightening.

Yet, at the same time, it strikes a fear into me that I realize I cannot even remotely express . . .

But is it really like this? I have spent two days . . .

After I read these pages, after I had numbered them, I also corrected them here and there, crossed out a few mistakes, even rewrote a few lines. I don't know why I did it, given that I had decided to push these inside Parini's head too.

In the end I rolled them up carefully, one by one, tilted the plaster bust, and began sliding them in. The first sheets went in easily, then, as the cavity gradually filled up, I had to push them in, and who knows how squashed and crumpled they became as they pressed together in there, being pushed against the strips of paper already inside toward the top of the head. Before feeding in the last sheet, I had to push a ballpoint pen into the hole and press hard two or three times to make some space.

Then I began to write these things.

Almost five years have gone by. I'm writing with a ballpoint pen. The ink of black berries I had collected in an inkwell is now unusable: it has separated and there's a kind of bluish liquid on top that leaves no mark on the paper, whereas a dark slimy residue has sunk to the bottom. I tried to stir it, but now the two parts won't mix any longer.

The Signorina died yesterday. For a long while she couldn't get out of bed, the flesh on her back had torn at several points. Each evening they lowered her nightdress to bathe the ulcers. They had bought a special bed for her, with parts that moved to stop bedsores forming. It was much higher than the previous one, with a metal tubular mechanism at the end, which made the blue room look completely different. The somber wallpaper, torn here and there, the picture of Mary Magdalene, the chest of drawers, and all the other objects in the room now seemed insignificant, almost unworthy compared with that large metal bed, whose chrome reflected the only weak source of light in the room: the light bulb that now hung outside its glass shade over the Signorina's head. At the side of the bed, in the same small circle of light, an oxygen bottle had also recently come to be added. It wasn't one of those small enamel bottles that are sometimes seen by the beds of the dying, but was tall, rusty, just like those used on construction sites. In fact, it was brought into the room by two men in overalls. But the mask placed over the Signorina's face every now and then was small, brand-new, of clear shiny plastic, and around it was the cellophane wrapping that kept it looking like new. The gas bottle and the mask were operated by an elderly nurse who spent the night at the Signorina's bedside. She was sparing in her use of the oxygen, would wait far too long, and to me, who watched her as she studied the Signorina's face on the point of suffocation, with her hand wavering over the valve of the gas bottle to gain one last second, her old eyes seemed to betray a fierce and smug hint of superiority.

Near the oxygen bottle there was also a coatrack, the same one that had frightened me several years ago. The bottle of the intravenous drip hung from one of its arms.

I continued going into the blue room until the very last. I sat down on the couch to study, to read, or simply to daydream. Before the Signorina lost consciousness, a priest would come once a week to bring her Communion. He would climb up the stairway, pass from one room to another and into the blue room. From a fold in his robe he would pull out a tiny pyx in the form of a case. I watched from the far end of the room: it was a small gold object he kept in his pocket and, by pressing a button, clicked open like certain kinds of powder compact. There are similar devices on various pieces of furniture in the house. The priest took a consecrated host and raised it up. I glimpsed a white reflection inside the small lid of the case, and from this I could see it contained other hosts. The Signorina waited for the host with her mouth open, holding her dry, pointed tongue, blood-red with tiny sores, unnecessarily far out. The priest shut the case and returned it to his pocket, retraced his steps across the room and down the stairway. I often went with him to the door at the bottom and several times was on the point of asking him to let me have a closer look at the case, to see how it opened, how it was made inside. Or even whether he would give it to me because I could think of several small things I could hide inside it.

One day the Signorina had insisted that someone hurry off to call the confessor. But no one paid any attention: she had confessed just two days before, they said, and had received Communion just the previous day, so what need was there? But the Signorina insisted so much, crying and banging the bed with her shriveled hands, that she eventually got her way. I went myself to call the confessor, and I remember it wasn't easy to persuade him to come. What sins could she have committed in those two days, the confessor said with a smile on his lips. She needn't worry, he knew her sins! I had to work hard to persuade him. Finally he took his stole, folded it several times, slipping it beneath his arm, and came. I walked along the road with him, but as soon as he entered the blue room and sat down beside the Signorina's bed, putting on his stole with a stern expression, I had to leave the room. I stopped for a few moments in the anteroom, but from there I could hear nothing. The confessor spent a long time with the Signorina that day, and when I accompanied him down the stairway I could see he was tense, silent, almost raging.

During her last days, before receiving the intravenous drip, the Signorina was fed with a spoon. They piled several pillows behind her head, putting the food into her mouth with an old silver teaspoon used only for her. They put liquids into a feeding bottle, from which she was able to suck even after she had lost consciousness, at the start of her long death.

On the last occasion she used it, I was the one who took it to her. But first, without being seen, I opened it and added a heaped teaspoonful of coffee. I shook it firmly as I approached the blue room so that the coffee powder would mix in. I put the bottle to the mouth of the Signorina, who for ten days had been unable to recognize anyone. She took hold of it with both hands, began to suck, but after a few moments she stopped and frowned, then her face completely relaxed. Turning toward me with infinite surprise she waved her hand several times in the air, groping in search of something.

The commode had been taken from the room some time before and in its place was a new armchair on which those who came to visit could sit. I often saw a long bedpan being taken around the house, covered with a page of a newspaper, which left a fetid trail in the rooms through which it passed.

Throughout these years I continued digging in the courtyard, though less often than before. So far, I have filled twelve jars in all and, since there was no more room on the shelf, I have put some on a small table in my room by the old couch where I used to lie listening to the enormous radio close by.

The Signorina's last days were awful. She shouted, pulled the bedclothes off with a force quite unimaginable, sat up in bed struggling to push the nurse away as she tried to get up. Sometimes I had to rush there too, and both of us had difficulty pinning that body, so light and withered, to the bed. She seemed frantic, fought with her arms, shouted horrible things, tried to bite with her toothless gums.

Something like this happened two days ago while I was alone with her in the blue room. I had gone in while they were changing the bedsheets, which were soiled with urine and feces. They had rolled up the dirty sheets and were carrying the great bundle away through the rooms. Having exposed her back, they bathed her ulcers. There was a basin by the bed, and they drew the water from it with a sponge. They covered her up again and, before going off with the basin and the dirty linen, they asked me to keep an eye on her until they returned.

I was sitting by her bed. The Signorina seemed perfectly calm under the folded blanket. I could smell the droplets of perfume they had put into her neatly combed hair, which was thin though still black. I was gazing at her, pensively, when, with a violent tug that took me completely by surprise, the Signorina managed to pull off the bedclothes that had been tucked under the mattress, causing them to fly to one side. I didn't know what to do. I pressed her shoulders with my hands to keep her down. I could feel her bones quavering and pressing against the palms of my hands. Suddenly she began to shout, hitting my face and shoulders. I pushed her down even further onto the bed with the whole force of my body. But all at once, I can't explain how, the Signorina managed to leap free and, throwing herself to one side, put her legs down from the bed. She was shouting that she wanted to get up. I begged her to stay down, but she kept hitting me. So I took hold of her arms, throwing her back on the bed. She started shouting even louder, made threats, wanting to cause trouble. She kept trying to get up and, in the struggle, was throwing her legs about to get a grip. Her nightdress had risen up to her stomach and, as she struggled to break free, trying to touch the surface of the bed with her feet, she kicked out, violently splaying her legs. She did it two or three times, under my eyes, and I could hardly avoid seeing among the sparse hairs below her stomach, in the middle of a kind of swelling, a grayish crack, almost black, with traces of blood beneath.

I pushed her down more forcefully, I may even have struck her. I too was shouting, as loud as I could, to cover her voice. "Keep down, damn you!" I shouted, and meanwhile I became aware to my horror that a deep sexual excitement was welling up inside me.

All the others ran to the room on hearing the shouts, along with the nurse. They took over the struggle, while I ran from the blue room.

I climbed onto the roof terrace, but only for a moment, as the clinic oven was in use and the wind was blowing the smoke toward me. I went down to dig in the courtyard, then returned to the house, where they told me the Signorina was very ill and might be about to die.

I shut myself in the bathroom, remaining there for a while, lost in thought, sitting on a corner of the bathtub. All of a sudden I leapt to my feet, my arms flailing in the air. A moment later my face was almost in the water, and one hand was in it, to halfway up my arm. I forgot to pull my sleeve up and it was all wet. There was a fish I couldn't catch, and it slipped out of my hand two or three times. Finally I managed to catch hold of it, just below its head, at its widest point, gripping it around its gills. I pulled it from the water, and it seemed to get gradually heavier as I lifted it up, as though it were made of lead. It wriggled about, flapped from side to side, arching itself, electric.

I'm not sure . . . Time passed. I knew this from the sky-light above. How strange, I had never noticed the skylight was there . . . I'd have liked to lie on the floor and stay there forever. But I had to go out, I had no idea what was going on in the house. There was a dead fish in the bath. A trace of blood was coming from its mouth. It was floating stiffly, up and down, tilting slightly to one side, cutting uncon-sciously across the path of other fish that swam clear of it, unperturbed.

The doctor came and stayed for a long while in the blue room. The Signorina was trembling continuously, muttering incomprehensible phrases. I went and lay on the old couch in my room. I switched on the radio, and as I listened I could feel the tension inside me gradually subsiding. I began to yawn, then remained half asleep for quite some while. When I opened my eyes again it was already dark. My face was soaked and I couldn't understand why. I had my head and legs up on the arms of the couch, which was too short for anyone to lie stretched out.

I went back to the bathroom. I watched the fish swimming calmly in the bathtub, taking in mouthfuls of water. They moved their fins and tails and glided past each other, never touching. The dead fish was no longer there, someone must have already removed it.

I let another few hours go by, I don't remember how, then went to bed without eating, and at the end of that long night filled with voices, sounds, and footsteps, the Signorina died.

I rushed into the blue room. There was a circle of people around the bed. On the floor, motionless among the succession of feet, shone the aluminum color of the tortoise.

"It's all over!" someone said, turning toward me.

I left. I started wandering the rooms. Every so often I saw someone appear from the corridor or from the stairway, since all the doors of the house had been opened. They hurried about. Someone opened the wrong doors in haste and wandered aimlessly for a while before finding the blue room. Someone else, mistaking me for a lost visitor, muttered a few ungenerous words about those who lived in the house. All these people, it seemed to me, moved around the rooms discourteously, peered everywhere, stopped to finger certain ornaments. All at once I saw a nun dressed in white. As she crossed the anteroom our eyes met and I recognized her: she's the one who loads the clinic oven. I think she recognized me too: more than once, looking up from the oven, she must have seen me standing in the fork of the tree with the black berries.

I went into the bathroom and sat on a corner of the bathtub. Now and then, outside, I could hear the hurried thud of feet resonating on the three wooden steps between the kitchen and the corridor. The fish behind me stirred the water lightly with their tails. After a while, once the coming and going had begun to subside, I changed position so as to be more comfortable. I crouched on the floor and stretched my arms along the edges of the bathtub, resting my cheek on the small enameled space that juts out of the corner. I had my face close to the water and watched the heads of the fish as they drew in mouthfuls of water, passing under my eyes in their continual rotation. I watched their methodical mouths, their eyes that betrayed not the slightest emotion. A more rapid flip of the tail as they passed round the curve beneath me was the only sure sign that they could see my large face looming somewhat distorted beyond the surface of the water.

I got up and left the bathroom. Returning to the blue room, I could see there were still many people around the bed of the Signorina, onto whom they had put a dress I had never seen her wear and, to hide her feet deformed by arthritis, a pair of new shoes too tight, which she had never managed to fit in when she was alive.

I wandered around the house again and after a while, quite suddenly, remembered I had seen the glint of something around the Signorina's bed, at a point very high up in the room. I hadn't managed to study it for more than a second, and yet I was sure it was the metal spokes of a bicycle wheel.

I went up to the roof terrace. Looking down from above, the courtyard seemed at the foot of a sheer drop. The terrace floor is on a slope and, unless you are lying flat on the ground trying to avoid rolling down, you have to grip on to the rusty rail hoping it doesn't come loose from its brittle base at the first touch.

I lay down on the ground without even looking across to the hole of the gutter. I undid my trousers to have a look: my penis was dark and bleeding slightly. A little later I went back down to the kitchen. No one was there, but there was a line of dishes on the table with no cloth. Some had food in them; others, empty, were dirty at the bottom, indicating that someone, in the confusion of those past few hours, had already eaten. I ate something too.

I don't remember what else I did for the rest of the day. I know that I continued wandering the house amid the coming and going of people, which further increased in the afternoon. Two men came toward evening to take away the oxygen bottle, which they carried horizontally through the rooms, with the risk at every step of hitting a glass door or a piece of furniture. On the stairway it slipped out of their grasp, rolling down a whole flight of steps. It bounced down with an enormous clatter, so that the valve nearly flew off at every thud and the oxygen almost escaped and filled the whole vastness of the stairway in an instant.

I went to the bedroom with the sheepskin cover and took the hunting horn down from the wall. I gave it three mighty blasts.

People arrived in the evening too, until eleven, when all the doors were shut. During the night a small group remained in the blue room. I could hear their voices even from my room and couldn't sleep. I got out of bed, opened a window, and looked out, gazing for a while without seeing anything. Little by little I thought I could smell a sickening odor in the air. I had an immediate suspicion. I began to peer into the darkness, over the metal fence that divides the court-yard of the house from that of the clinic, toward the area of the oven. I couldn't detect any smoke, though my eyes were slowly adjusting to the dark. Perhaps something was moving, though it could be a simple optical effect caused by my continual staring at the mesh of the metal fence. I turned away for a while and when I looked back I realized there was a light object in front of the oven. I glimpsed a movement. Perhaps it was a nun, one of the nurses, crouched in front of the metal opening, busily loading the oven in the dark-ness. Or perhaps there were two. I flapped my arm several times, as if to shoo away an animal, and there seemed to be a kind of scuttling away from the oven. So I wasn't wrong! I searched about for some object on the furniture. The first thing I came across was an alarm clock. I hurled it from the window and over the metal fence with a high lob. When it dropped into the clinic courtyard, I'm not sure where but some distance from the oven, the light object moved: two nuns, nurses, stood up and remained motionless in full view, in front of me. I looked for something else in the room. As I was lifting a small but heavy marble bust from the table, a small-scale reproduction of the head of a Greek general, Alcibiades I believe, my foot knocked against something. I bent down and realized straightaway it was the tortoise. Its bright shell, caught in the dim nocturnal light that came in through the window, could be distinguished even in the near total darkness of the room. I took hold of it. A few seconds later it was over the fence. I heard a metallic noise from the direction of the oven: perhaps it had hit the oven door and its shell had been smashed. Straight after, I hurled the small marble bust. The two nuns began shrieking and ran off with their heads down, along the path from the oven to the glass door of the clinic.

I stayed at the window for quite some time to make sure the nuns didn't come out again thinking I had gone back to bed. From above, I began to recognize the intricate, impenetrable outline of the hawk's hedge in the darkness. My eyes now began even to distinguish the large stone, which seemed to become gradually brighter in the darkness, as though it contained phosphorescent substances. "How could I've never noticed?" I thought. Not even when I was learning to ride a bicycle and went back and forth over it until dusk and sometimes late into the evening. I used to sit on the lowest part of the frame of an old bicycle with a low crossbar that women use, onto which I put a cushion to make it more comfortable. I held my legs out wide and straight so that, although they were short, they wouldn't touch the ground and so that, when I picked up speed on the short descent from the stone, I wouldn't collide with something and hurtle off. I held my arms up to grip the handlebars, which were higher than my head. I pushed myself along for a while, then glided down the short descent to learn how to keep my balance. I was careful not to fall off on the stone itself because it would have broken every bone.

It was already evening when I put the bicycle back in the garage. I enjoyed getting into the car, slamming the door, and sitting there inside. I even managed to get in when I found it completely wrapped. I lifted the cloth cover, pulling the elastic at the bottom just enough to open the door, and worked my way in through the gap, keeping the door firm with one elbow so that it didn't close too fast under the pressure of the elastic. I used to spend a long time sitting there. No one, not even anyone who happened to be in the garage and just a few inches from the car, would have imagined I was there so close. It was all dark. Just a few patches, where the cloth was worn, allowed some light to filter through to give some idea of the interior of the car. I put my hands on the dashboard . . . there, we were off to the sea and the car had an incredible load on the roof and the wind was making it sway like a sail, swerving suddenly from one side of the road to the other. There was also the risk of getting stopped by the police because the car didn't have the proper wheels, they were aircraft wheels that could be found cheaply in certain places at the end of the war. Sitting next to me was the Signorina, who spent the whole journey cooling herself with a Venetian fan they had given her as a present. I often took it from her, opened and closed it endlessly to work out how it could so suddenly change shape and size, concertina-ing, closing onto itself and then suddenly folding out on its wooden slats.

At the seaside, the Signorina rarely went down to the beach. They chose the early hours of the afternoon for her, when no one was about. She wore an old-fashioned black bathing costume that ended with a tiny pleated skirt, like a tutu. A man, the driver, lifted her and took her in his arms over the whole scorching sand like this, carrying her to where the sea began and beyond, where the water reached waist height. Suddenly the Signorina slipped out of the driver's arms and started swimming with unexpected agility. She threw her head back, plunging into the water to wet her hair. She surfaced again and her hair glistened like silk against the background of the empty sun-drenched sea . . .

I shut the window and went back to bed. But after a while I got up again. I dressed and began to wander around the rooms. Several drowsy voices could still be heard in the blue room. I turned along the corridor. Passing under the iron bar, I jumped up, took hold of it, and did several pull-ups. I went into the kitchen, intending to sit by the stove. But it had gone cold and, on opening the door, I saw there was only ash. I didn't know what to do. I went into the small study, opened a few drawers, then thought of climbing up to the roof terrace. I had never been up there at night. I paused for a while, then began to push the heavy iron door, sliding it along its tracks. Climbing up the rusty ladder, I tackled the steps one by one in the dark. On reaching the roof terrace, I lay straight down on the floor at a right angle to the slope so as not to roll down against the low powdery wall that held the railing. I turned my head toward the hole in the gutter: behind the glass door of the clinic, two light patches shimmered, moved apart then back together. They might have been simple reflections of light coming from inside. I continued watching in that direction for quite some while. Suddenly two nuns emerged from the glass door. I was almost above their heads, I could see them as they moved surreptitiously, looking toward the window of my room. They crossed the stretch of courtyard, suspecting nothing, pushing a trolley, and approached the oven to load it. "Perhaps there have been many operations over the past few days," I thought, "and they accumulated such a mass of stuff that, to dispose of it, they have to work the oven even at night. Or maybe they've begun burning stuff from other clinics too . . ." There was nothing on the roof that I could throw down to frighten them, apart from my body. I could have jumped up and shouted at them from the darkness of the terrace to frighten them away. I lay there, instead, and after a while I sensed that smell in my nostrils. Even though the night was dark and the sky filled with clouds heaped like sacks of garbage, I could make out a few whorls of smoke as they passed against the only slight glimmer to be seen in one part of the atmosphere. I didn't feel like getting up and seeing the courtyard at the foot of the precipice, with the last fragment of luminous stone that jutted out. It was dangerous to put my hands on the railing since the parapet could crumble and the railing might come loose, like a tooth from an old gum. A slight wind blew up, I felt a chill on my face. Every now and then, from the highway beyond the courtyard of the clinic, I could hear the milk trucks that began to pass by at this very hour.

When I was younger I would often look out from the railing and, one day, was on the point of throwing myself down, sure that I would have dropped slowly and, if I flapped my arms a few inches before landing, would gently touch the ground. Maybe I could have flown up and over the hawk's hedge and then the tree with the black berries and then the metal fence and the clinic roof. Meanwhile, in a corner of the courtyard, several snails I was testing out were struggling to climb onto a framework built inside a basin, an intricate pyramid of small branches that I kept constantly wet because water, by diluting the snail slime, made them fall off. Those that reached the top were safe. I set them free on some leaves in the middle of the hawk's hedge, with a colored mark painted on their shell. This small indication prevented the snail from being put a second time into the bowl for the test. Many marks of varying shape and color had therefore begun to move about and congregate inside the hawk's hedge, crawling over the roots and into the dense darkness of the foliage.

And if I had gone to the railing again and climbed over it? I could have stood there, above the courtyard and, on seeing it from high up, small and black like the mouth of a well, I could have made out the luminous rock as far as its farthest limits that spread out under the ground, like in an X-ray, I could have flown over the top of the clinic roof passing through the smoke of the oven, and then encountered great empty spaces, floating high above other courtyards, looking through windows like the portholes of sunken ships . . .

I think I must have fallen asleep for a while, and realized I was completely frozen. The small glow in the sky had opened up, perhaps because of the wind. And inside, it was full of stars. The last whorls of smoke from the oven passed in front of it and seemed to rise up into it. I wanted to stand up and go back down to the house but felt incapable of doing so. I tried to sit up. First I had to turn onto my side, leaning forward and crawling on the floor, then with a sudden jerk I managed to pull myself up. Beyond the roof of the house, in the opposite direction of the clinic, I seemed to see, in the center of a large piazza not far away, several presences, vast and immobile, like scaffolding, around which many infinitely small men moved about in the semidarkness. I couldn't figure out what they were. I tried to pull myself up, but failed after several attempts and lay back down on the floor. I had no choice but to sleep there. And perhaps I would never wake up again.

When I reopened my eyes it was daytime. I realized to my horror that I had ended up against the base of the railing. Perhaps, as I slept, I had rolled down without being aware of it. I had to move back straightaway, before the parapet collapsed. But I couldn't move. Propping myself on my elbows, I managed to crawl a couple of yards along the floor. Lifting my head I could see that the piazza was crowded with people, flags, symbols, vast banners. A line of men had gathered shoulder to shoulder, as though facing up to the crowd, on an enormous platform on which there were clusters of loudspeakers. A moment later, loud music started up. I heard no sound coming from the crowd, though it seemed as if the whole piazza, at that very moment, had given out a sigh, as though an immense, invisible air bubble had formed. After a while a voice began to blare out, spreading from the center of the platform and echoing through the whole piazza like an enormous shell, while the crowd gradually went still. A dense black smoke, perhaps from a bonfire, started to rise up from one part of the piazza. There was applause. The wind blew the first rapid wisps of smoke until they passed over the terrace. The clinic oven, having worked through the night, was still and lifeless, with its door open, and seemed to have gone out.

I tried to get up and succeeded after many attempts. I was cold and stiff, and felt a constant urge to vomit. Climbing down the rusty ladder I gripped the rail so as not to fall onto the roof and, by rolling over it, crash down into the anteroom through the skylight.

The stove in the kitchen was already lit. I sat down beside it and let my face drop onto an elbow a few inches from its red-hot rings until I began to feel the heat enter my frozen head, as far as my brain, through my brows, and to cook my eyes, which were as hard and cold as two bits of bone. I suddenly heard a sizzle: a lock of hair had touched the rings, burning immediately.

After a while I got up. I wandered around the rooms. I was amazed to see that the tortoise was back in the house: it was unharmed and making its way toward the blue room. I shut myself in my room and began writing these things.

I don't know what I'll do now. I reckon I'll quit the house.

I've decided to put these last sheets of paper into Parini. I'll look for some metal and press down the paper that's already inside to make some space. I'll squash and compress it as far as I can. I'll go now and see . . .

On tilting the plaster head I discovered that a strip of paper is now poking from the opening, like a small tail. Not that it is actually sticking out, but if you look into the hole it's impossible not to see it. Since the paper is already packed down, I'm afraid that someone, by holding the tip of that appendage and carefully pulling, might manage to extract the whole contents, unraveling them from the cavity of the head. As soon as I've put these sheets of paper in as well, I'll have to take care that none of it sticks out at all, because the great quantity of compressed paper inside could begin to expand and even push up the plaster head, tilting it, tipping it over the banister, causing it to crash down to the foot of the stairs. With a piece of metal I'll push these bits of paper down too, as far as possible, until I hear the scrunch of the paper pressed down to occupy the last tiny remaining empty spaces. Already, once before, I happened to notice that small unlikely spaces in the head, which I had believed to be absolutely full, come free when the paper, on being pressed down really hard, passes through minuscule passages and manages to occupy even the inner part of the nose and certain empty and barely accessible recesses of the ear.

Before returning to my room, I went into the blue room for a moment. The Signorina is still there, still lying in exactly the same position as yesterday evening. It has begun to rain outside and water is coming in through one corner of the room. It seeps through the middle of a damp patch on the ceiling and drips down onto the floor. The tortoise was heading toward that point. Something in its slowness made me think it was racing at breakneck speed. It stretched its wrinkled snout toward the drops of water, trying to drink.

But it stretched too far and several drops landed on its head, its shell, and its eyes. So it immediately withdrew.

Once I've pushed these sheets of paper inside the head, I thought I could pour some alcohol into the opening and set fire to it. But maybe the fire would go out immediately, choked by the lack of air and by the compressed paper, hard and impenetrable as cement, or maybe it would ignite the sculpted head, turning the plaster into a red-hot ball. The combustion might cause the skull or the face of that immobile head to explode at some point, scattering around it pieces of paper that hadn't fully burned and which someone might manage to decipher here and there . . .

I think I've found the answer: if I can't manage to prevent something from poking out of the hole, then I'll stop it all up with a bullet.

I'll go check whether it's possible.

Yes, it is. The bullet is slightly wider than the opening, but only by very little. Once I've filled the head, I'll push the bullet into the opening, a little at a time, tapping it gently with a hammer, and when it's properly inside, perfectly in line with the plinth, no one will ever manage to get it out. It will look like a tiny metal disk and everyone will think it has always been part of the statue.

The Hole

In the middle there was a circular hole, black and steaming, molded into the cement.

Squatting over it, the child looked out of the little window or whirled a small spinning top in front of him to pass the time. When he realized the excrement was about to drop, falling onto other swollen excrement inside the hole, his mother's who had just died in childbirth, or the wet nurse's, or his first granddad's, he covered his ears so as not to hear the sound. He couldn't bear the relentless sound of excrement dropping on top of excrement, and especially the sound of urine that splashed onto it inside the hole, because his penis and the feces could always be joined through the electrical channel of the urine, and then all the feces contained in the hole would instantly return back up into his penis.

Nor could he spit in there, into the hole. If he really had to, he would close his eyes so as not to see, and would then run off into the vegetable patch, taking care not to stumble over those great big stinging nettles. The Signora used to go walking at the bottom of the vegetable patch. She wore an old-fashioned dress down to her feet. A cushion tied around her kidneys kept her skirt raised, forming a large saddle that the child would have liked to leap onto if the Signora hadn't already once clouted him, cutting his face with her ring.

He stood up and, when it was already dark, he lit the stub of a candle that sat upright in the little window beside the box of kitchen matches. He poured a bucket of water in, then put the wooden lid on the hole. The excrement, meanwhile, pressing itself down, would be gradually sinking into a shocking intimacy. The flame of the candle flickered over the hole, caught by an imperceptible waft of air.

He went out and crossed the vegetable patch, walking around the nettles. Hanging from a wall of the house was a section of ladder held up by two large nails, one of which went right through into his room, emerging by the head of his bed. With a leap, the child grabbed the first rung and climbed up to the top. With his back to the wall, he climbed down and back up two or three times along that ladder that went nowhere. "How small I've become," he thought as he noted how the rungs seemed farther and farther apart. From up there he could see the Signora strolling at the bottom of the vegetable patch with her large saddle, the first granddad, who was writing on a table with its legs half sunk in the ground, and, looking diagonally through the small window, the perfect circle of the hole, impassive in the stench.

It looked as if it had been traced out by a pair of compasses. "How did they manage it?" the boy wondered. Maybe, to get such a perfect circumference, they had stuck a metal tube into the cement while it was still fresh, had marked around it several times before cutting it out. And maybe one of the builders had had an irresistible urge to put his mouth to the other end of the tube, shouting or singing for the simple pleasure of hearing his voice amplified. Then they must have put the layer of cement onto the old base of beaten ground, placing the circumference of the new hole exactly on top of the old one.

The new floor sloped slightly toward the middle, and the hole swallowed up everything. Not just the bucketfuls of water that were poured down, but also marbles that sometimes fell out of his pocket as he squatted, and the small spinning top too. It always ended up right by the hole, dancing along its edge. And certain small animals went in there too, flies and ants, as well as two snails that seemed quite at home. He had seen them crawl around its walls, retreat into their shells and fall asleep, hanging there inside, offering the minimal possible resistance to the floods of water poured down from the bucket above. There were also mice that sometimes leapt out unexpectedly, brushing their ears against his little scrotum. They forced him always to keep well clear, for fear that they might nibble him. He had also seen bees go down there to make honey, several summer fireflies, and once, when he got up very early one morning, two large multicolored butterflies. He bent down to take a better look at them: their bodies were locked together and they seemed to be in ferocious combat. They were making screeching sounds while bits of their wings broke off and they wheeled down toward the bottom of the hole.

In there, however, you could also find blood, garbage, chicken entrails. Then the cats, sniffing the smell from far off, would jump into the outhouse through the window, drop their gnashing heads into the hole. You could also find eggshells, broken beakers, leftover balls of wool of all colors. It all sank down and reemerged long after, when nobody even remembered it.

In summertime, under the wooden lid, the hole festered. But in the winter, if you looked down over its frozen edge, you could see and recognize every object like in an icy urn. Sometimes, as he was squatting there with his eyes shut, the boy seemed to remember that the old floor of beaten earth had been very different from the new one, that it didn't slope toward the middle, that the hole was in fact slightly raised, like a crater. And that, once the hole had filled to the top, two great arms held it suspended in the air while it emptied. "Who knows," he wondered, "whether the old floor was still there beneath the new one? Who knows whether between those two sloping surfaces there is still a gap?" He got up to take a look. He put one foot on the floor and pedaled against the wall with the other, expecting the whole outhouse to start rotating upon itself, like a merry-go-round, pivoted on the fixed circle of the hole.

He went back to the outhouse before going to bed, and then it really was completely dark. He was frightened at the thought of urinating onto the swelling of freshly dropped excrement. His stream of urine was drilling into it. Whose was it? He lit the candle, tilted it, held it very close so that he could recognize it. Large drops of candle wax fell into the hole and began to sink like everything else toward the center of the earth. There was total silence, and yet he could hear a distant whirling there inside. The wax kept slowly sinking. A churning sound rose from the depth. He closed the hole with the lid. "Who knows why it has to be sealed so tightly?" he wondered. Would all the animals and objects come out? What happened in there at night, when the lights were suddenly switched on beneath the crust of the earth? He pushed the lid down with his foot until the sounds came to a complete halt. Then he blew out the candle.

Back in his room, he undressed, hanging his clothes on the short tip of the nail that jutted from the wall, between the mortar and the river stones. He was careful when he turned his head on the pillow so that it wouldn't stick into his face. On the floor above, the footsteps of the wet nurse made the floorboards shake, you could see them sagging and then returning to their place, supported by the large beams.

But it was enough for a shoe to fall, for a marble to bounce, or even for the cat to scamper lightly and silently about, and the floor above his head would start sounding again as if by magic. He could hear his newborn baby brother crying in his crib. There, that slight shaking of the whole house meant that the wet nurse had gone to him, had lifted him up high, drawing him close to her distorted face to comfort him. The baby started immediately to suck, tugging with such a frenzy as to shake all the windows of the house. The wet nurse meanwhile kept her eyes fixed on the mirror, stared at the little fragrant head that was so readily emptying her with his tiny rubber lips.

Then the noises stopped but, if you listened carefully, something continued to make the house softly vibrate. Maybe it was the slow breathing of those asleep, maybe the last roaming vibrations from the large radio switched off two hours earlier. Silently, the outhouse closed its eyes in the atavistic night. Beneath the wooden lid, the hole was impassively digesting. The little boy muttered a few words in the dark to make sure he still remembered them. In his mind he went through the consonants and the vowels. He stretched out his arm and touched the tip of the nail beneath his clothes. He had the feeling that if he gave it a slight pull with his hand it would fly out of the wall in an instant and the ladder outside the house would drop into the night with all the animals roosting on it. On the side wall, above the door, he could make out the shadow of an old framed coat of arms.

He pictured in his mind the Arab head above it, immobile between two long ornamental leaves. "Who knows why the wet nurse has a distorted face?" he wondered. Meanwhile, he searched with his hand for the polystyrene ball he kept under one corner of the pillow, all that remained of the head of a musical owl. He took hold of the small metal ring that stuck out. He pulled it hard, releasing a long cord.

And as the music box began to play its little tune, always the same, and the cord gradually recoiled into the head, even before the music had come to an end, he felt he was at last falling asleep.

The boy had three grandfathers.

The first lived in the house, which he had built himself with stones from the river. He worked at the public truck scale and, in his spare time, copied passages from famous works into large bound notebooks, arranging the topics in alphabetical order so as to create an encyclopedia. He strolled around the vegetable patch, went to write on the table whose legs were half buried in the ground. Before sitting down he moved the seeds that were spread there to dry, heaped them all to the sides to make room for one of his large open notebooks, its title embossed in gold on the spine.

When he went to the truck scale, the boy often secretly followed him. He waited until the trucks that parked on the large metal platform drove off before he ran all over it. He peeped toward his first granddad's cabin and waited to see him leave the dials inside and appear at the tiny window as soon as he realized the boy was there. But the platform didn't drop down at all, not even if he took a run-up and gave a loud shout, leaping onto it from a great height. "It's no use, I'm still too little . . ." he could only conclude, standing immobile in the center of the platform.

The second granddad had one fingernail longer than the others and lived in a large villa that had once belonged to a musician. The boy waited each day at the gate without entering. The second granddad came out, always at the same time, with his walking stick. He walked slowly, but sometimes they went as far as the large sidewalk that crossed the end of the street, where men squatted to draw with chalk. Halfway along the route they sat on a bench in front of which the public carriages stopped while the horses ate from their feedbags. They listened to the sound of the glossy jaws chewing hay, or hard oats in the shallower bags. Walking down a long avenue, the second granddad spiked all the fallen leaves he could see with the point of his stick. He stabbed them in the middle with a single musical stroke, secured them more firmly by pushing the point a little harder into the ground. Gradually, as he progressed, the leaves compacted against each other, rising up toward the handle of the stick like a great segmented caterpillar.

"Tell me an Arab name!" the boy asked him one of those days while they were pacing out the exceptional length of an American automobile parked at one side of the street.

The second granddad frowned.

"Abd!" he replied at last.

They remained silent for a while. All they could hear was the dry thuds of the walking stick piercing each leaf in exactly the same part of its thin veins.

The third granddad lived who knows where. The boy saw him from time to time for just a few moments, sitting on his gig, singing, whipping his horse as it trotted along. He moved fast, hurtled down the hills. His legs were always covered by a woolen check blanket, and the boy, glimpsing his face between the revolving spokes, hearing the crack of the whip and the wild creaking of the wheels and the beating of the hooves that sent out sparks, would have liked more than anything in the world to have paralyzed legs, like the third granddad.

"Abd!" he thought, once he had climbed onto the section of ladder while the little dog Isabel watched him anxiously from below, waiting for him to come down. In the vegetable patch, the first granddad was writing a letter for a man who was illiterate and had been standing there waiting for quite a while. "Abd," the boy repeated to himself, "perhaps his name really was Abd . . ." The dog, getting impatient, began barking to make him come down.

One day, as he walked along the avenue with the second granddad, the boy returned to the subject.

"Is Abd really an Arab name?"

"Of course!"

"And how did Abd manage to get as far as here?"

The second granddad raised the point of his stick.

"That's simple," he replied after a moment. "He came here from Spain, for sure."

"And to get to Spain, where did he come from?"

"Well . . . maybe from the Berber tribes of the Sahara desert, or from Ghazna or Cairo, from Baghdad or much farther away, from the ancient regions of Mesopotamia or even from the Urals . . ."

"And how is he dressed?"

"Oh . . . he has a lance, a double-bladed ax, a pike, a cudgel, sword and dagger, bow, arrows, and an oryx-skin shield. He's covered all over by a surcoat of chain mail, and on his head he also has a fine chain mail hood."

"And what's he like?"

"He's dark-skinned, almost Black, has slanting eyes and a flat nose."

"Go on . . ."

"The Arabs pass through Toledo, Seville, Andalusia, Castile, they capture Málaga. The warriors march in great parades in front of the Caliph, displaying their spoils and trophies . . ."

"Does Abd know the Caliph?"

"Of course! He marched with the other warriors too, and the Caliph saw him just for an instant among a thousand men, but was struck by his appearance . . . They advance, press on through the Pyrenees, as far as Bordeaux, into France, and to Poitiers, Avignon, Lyon, while the Caliph's army keeps increasing its number of Slav mercenaries . . ."

The second granddad suddenly stopped. Bending slightly, he spiked a small green leaf that had just fallen to the ground. The child squeezed his hand more firmly so that he would carry on with the story.

"We've arrived!" the second granddad said, looking up. As they were talking, they had indeed arrived at the boy's house. The second granddad went for a moment to the outhouse. Standing over the hole, with a quick movement of his hand, he slipped the sheath of leaves off the stick.

After he had gone, the child went into the outhouse. He dropped his trousers and, as he was defecating onto the crackling mass of leaves, to pass the time he took the small bubble pot and began blowing . . .

What were the ships like? They certainly had an infinity of oars and large sails, and the crew were packed together like animals, ready to leap across the strait. The armored heads of the warriors glistened in the sun for miles. Abd's head too. They waited for the shout to depart. Then an invisible man moved a finger, imperceptibly, inside one of the ships, and an immense shout beat against the sky, taut as the skin of a drum. The sea surged on every side, the blades of the oars smashed against the foam. The metallic heads leaned barbarically in the space. On his ship, under his colored turban, the invisible man closed his eyes like a stone in flight. Abd's eyes searched the depths of the sky, felt the frame of the ship rise under the thrust of enormous masses of moving water. His large beaked nose breathed boundlessly in the sea air . . .

How much time had passed? The child stood up reluctantly, only because his legs had pins and needles. He poured the bucket of water into the hole. He blew some more bubbles from the ring, watching them as they gradually sank downward. They glanced against each other without bursting, emitting luminous reflections while the curve of their circumference disappeared from sight. Some burst silently on the ground. The boy had learned how to take them with the ring as they floated, to blow them again and catch them once more. He could also rest them on the mouth of the small cylindrical pot and then push the whole soapy ring into them without making them burst. He could join several of them together, one after the other like tramcars, then sweep them all off into the air. He blew them away, caught them again, tapped them with the ring, and sent them up, blew again, and the bubbles came down clustering to the center, went into the hole all together. To see them better, he lit the end of the candle, though outside it still wasn't very dark. He knelt down at the edge of the hole to find out whether they were still intact down below. He lifted the flame over his head then lowered it. He stretched his arm right into the hole, and if he couldn't make out the bubbles it was certainly because just the effect of that faint light was enough to make them explode at once.

Having left the outhouse, the boy walked through the vegetable patch. As he passed the nettles, he paused with an air of defiance. He stopped still for a moment in front of the big leaves swaying in the breeze, then ran off. He went to lie on a terra-cotta seat molded into the shape of a couch, complete with cushion, half submerged in a corner of the vegetable patch. He shut his eyes and covered them with one hand because the green husks could always drop down from the great chestnut tree that hung over it and spike him in the face. He felt a dull pain in the bones of his head because the cushion was also made of terra-cotta . . . They crossed Spain, sending Visigoth heads flying with their two-edged axes, and the air brought sounds of iron and breaking bones, and cities opened their gates, and hidden eyes were focused on the oryx-skin shields that rippled in the evening haze, while hordes of Goths with their long flowing hair fled toward the horizon. Abd lay down beneath the night sky, could see the rickety wagons far off behind the lines, the still shapes of astronomers on top of the towers, architects and mathematicians with great wise turbans who measured the sides of the hills by torchlight. As he rode under the night stars, he could feel inside his chain mail hood, in some part of his surging mind, a hollow bursting sensation of time hurtling backward . . .

Before night, the boy went back to the outhouse. He

took the small cylindrical bubble pot from the window ledge. He pulled out the ring and blew into it. He put it back in the soapy water, blew again several times. He couldn't see the small spheres floating in the darkness of the outhouse but could feel their presence all the same, and his cheeks sometimes felt their impalpable caress as they burst on his face. Testing the ground with his feet, he approached the hole and began to urinate with his eyes shut. But there was something making a loud echo, as if the stream of urine were dropping onto the skin of a drum. The boy forced himself to stop urinating, closed his little penis with his hand to be safe. With the other, he struck a match against the wall and lit the candle. He peered into the hole: there were chicken innards. The boy blew out the candle and carried on urinating against the wall so that those objects wouldn't slowly slither up into his penis.

In bed, before getting the polystyrene ball to play, he listened for quite a while to the noise of the baby sucking. He had watched him before he went to bed, naked and squeezing the wet nurse's breast, as if taking it by force, with his little feet swirling round and round. The first grandfather, standing still in the doorway, stared at the large breast that seemed gradually to disappear into the baby's little mouth, swallowed by that little body which, unable to contain the whole of it, let a small bubble of it escape between the creases of its legs . . . Abd's head, static on the coat of arms, surveyed the burned-out city at the far end of the plain. The warriors, laden with trophies, had difficulty controlling the jewel-en-crusted horses. There was a large rostrum crammed with turbans that seemed to be piled one on top of the other. The smoke from the fire, carried by the wind, made the noses of the horses quiver. As he slowly approached the rostrum, Abd peered among the folds of the turbans. Crouching there in the middle, the invisible body of the Caliph absorbed all the surrounding space. Slav mercenaries shook their heads in front of Abd, jangling interminable necklaces coiled into the dusty locks of their hair. His body was laden with tro-phies too, and his horse's tail and mane were interwoven with long branches of coral, and still under his nails was the interminable hair of a woman he had dragged over the scorching stones of a road. The horse trotted high, its hooves sparked on the stones. And when at last, right in front of the rostrum, his eyes had passed, blankly, over something very smooth and very swollen, as terrible as a scrap of newly born flesh, he then raised himself up on the stirrups of his horse and in that same instant, inside the folds of the turban, a momentary thought had passed through the Caliph's head: "I will remember this June afternoon, and that man standing on the stirrups of his horse, and the blurred sight of his ride against this scrap of conquered sky!"

The child pulled the cord and, beneath the blanket, the small polystyrene head began to play. The ceiling shook lightly, perhaps because of the notes of the music box that fil-tered through the blankets and rose gently upward. A gentle scratching against the wall outside indicated that a flock of birds had perched on the ladder to sleep. The boy closed his eyes. He thought that inside the hole, among the mass of excrement, leaves, and entrails mixed together, the soap bubbles too were dropping intact toward the center of the earth.

Next morning he woke early. The first granddad, standing in front of a shelf holding a bowl of steaming milk, kept his ear to the large radio to listen to the news. But the voice was hard to hear. He turned the knob several times, with no success. It was a hot day. The boy took a walk around the vegetable patch, passed close to the nettle leaves with feigned indifference. The Signora wasn't yet there. Entering the outhouse he was surprised to see Isabel the dog standing fixed at the edge of the hole, her snout continually gyrating, following the spirals of two bees buzzing inside and planning perhaps to catch both with one bite, digging her teeth into their little bodies to get out all the honey.

The boy stood watching her for a while, then left the outhouse. He climbed the section of ladder, listening out: generally, at this hour, the third granddad passed behind the house, wheeling down the hill, cracking his whip. He reached a point very high up the ladder so that the sound of the gig, crossing the roof, would reach him sooner. But no sound came from the road that day.

Later, when he saw the second granddad at the gate of the villa, he asked him why.

"This I really don't know . . ." was his swift reply.

There was a very long silence.

"And Abd?" the boy asked again, after a pause.

The second granddad seemed suddenly to cheer up.

"He's running away."

"Why?"

"There's been the battle at Poitiers. The Arab army has been driven back beyond the Pyrenees . . ."

"Abd as well?"

"No, a few scattered groups have remained in France, rushing here and there pillaging, their ranks gradually diminishing. They go through cities like this . . ."

"And how does Abd manage to avoid being recognized?"

"He's removed his chain mail hood and in its place he has a cuirass made of strips of leather and felt. And he has thrown a great cloak over it."

Next morning the boy listened out once again from one of the top rungs of the ladder. The Signora appeared in the vegetable patch. Seated behind the table, the first granddad was drafting a written application, with his head to one side. Standing in front of him was a young man who wanted to leave for Australia as soon as he could. The wet nurse was feeding. The boy heard her cry out two or three times, he held his breath. No crack of a whip came from the road, no rumble of large wooden wheels hurtling down the hill, no clopping of hooves. In the outhouse there was much activity, the antennas of small snails jutted out from the edge of the hole, and one insect was busy killing another, depositing its eggs in its body. Inside, there were also a fish bone, fish guts cut out with scissors, and, above all, an air bladder still whole. The boy stretched his hand in and managed to grab it. Later, lying on the terra-cotta couch, he blew it up for a while, until a cat appeared all at once and bit straight into it, making it suddenly burst.

"He didn't go past today either . . ." he told the second grandfather, as they were walking along the avenue.

This time there was no reply. The second grandfather was walking slightly farther ahead, the point of his stick had let several very large leaves get away.

That evening, in the candlelight, the boy saw something sticking out from the hole. He knelt down at the edge and stretched out his hand: it was the end of a colored thread that poked out from the solid crust of feces. He took it with two fingers and began to pull. The thread must have been very long because, cutting the excrement, it kept emerging and uncoiling. The boy carried on pulling, and he soon discovered that all the thread he had pulled out was as tall as him. Standing at the edge of the hole, he held one end of it with his arm stretched as far as he could. He jumped up to pull it a little more. Then he stood still, no longer knowing what to do. To go any farther he'd have to touch the thread with his hand each time he pulled out another arm's-length worth or, at least, if he kept the hand holding the end of the thread very high, each length equal to the full span of both arms. But he would have dirtied his fingers like that . . . The boy stopped to think. First of all, if he wanted to use his other hand, he had to put the candle down on the window. This is what he did, but first he tipped it slightly so that the molten wax would fall onto the tips of his fingers. He waited until it was completely dry, and when he could feel his fingertips perfectly isolated, protected by that fragile coating of wax, he continued pulling the thread out little by little. He often leaned over the hole, since the end of the thread still hadn't come out. It was cutting through the excrement, every so often it seemed about to snap as it passed through a more solid mass, but it was enough to pull harder until it continued sliding out with ease. Every so often there were knots, and then the boy really was afraid the thread would break and suddenly fly into his face, or that all the contents of the hole would slowly start to rise up. New coils fell one onto another by his feet; he had to move his hands methodically so that the thread didn't start to wrap itself around his arms and his legs. It would then have been enough for a section of thread to suddenly drop inside the hole through some unexpected suction, it would have been enough for a small air pocket somewhere deep down in the hole to swallow his body and gradually absorb it.

He must have been there a long time: the whole candle had melted on the windowsill. The boy's arms were aching. He wanted to pause for a while but was afraid the hole might suck all the thread back in, unraveling the coils one after another. He thought of leaving the outhouse but without releasing the end of the thread, he thought of taking a short walk in the vegetable patch to stretch his legs and, still without losing his grip, of going into the house and upstairs to his room and then lying down on the bed. Before going to sleep he could have continued pulling the thread from the hole, one span after another and, even as he slept, his arm could have kept moving and pulling, while the thread, sliding in complicated crisscrosses around corners beyond the outhouse and around the trees in the vegetable patch as if on well-oiled metal wheels, slipping between the shutters of the closed doors and up the steps of the staircase, curving round his bedroom wardrobe, could have continued emerging from the deepest regions of the hole, coiling into perfect circles on his pillow. And when he woke, suddenly turning his head, he would have found the other end quietly sleeping beside him.

The flame flared up on the wick still lodged in a drop of molten wax. Still more knots appeared, then the fine, sharp thread began to slip out effortlessly once again, almost accelerating. When the other end finally emerged, the boy was now no longer expecting it. He continued pulling his arm in and out without realizing that his wax-coated fingers were pulling nothing. The other end of the thread lay on the ground beside the hole, with nothing attached, with no reel, without even completing the last circumference begun.

The boy eventually saw it beneath him. Quick as a flash he put the lid on the hole without looking inside. With one foot, he pushed all the thread into the corner of the outhouse so that it couldn't go back during the night to where it had been, lifting the lid or slithering slowly through one of its cracks. He was exhausted, his eyes continually falling shut. "I'll wash it tomorrow," he told himself as he left the outhouse, half asleep.

Next day, as soon as he woke and even before dressing, he ran down to see the thread: it was still there, even if its coils seemed to have grown slightly wider during the night, spreading farther over the floor. The boy carefully lifted his foot so as not to get dirty, then stepped inside. Gradually walking around, he studied it carefully from every angle. After he had dressed he went down again to wash it. He poured several buckets of water over it, then dropped it into an old brick drinking trough. He passed the whole thread through a handful of dust, washed it again, and, rewinding it, finally put it out to dry in the sun.

It was a long job: it took the whole morning. Meanwhile, he hadn't forgotten to listen out for the crack of the whip. But to no avail. Isabel, jealous of the attention she saw he was giving to the thread, had gone to lie down in the middle of the coils. The first granddad gave the radio a bang with his fist.

The boy went up to the room where the wet nurse and the baby were and stayed there for a while, on a pouf with wheels. When the wet nurse wasn't there, sitting on it, he pushed himself in all directions. He got it to move fast, lying on top of it with his face down, pedaling and pushing as hard as he could, steering with his hands on the floor. He hurtled around the room. The baby carried on sleeping soundly in his crib, ignoring the squeaking of the wheels.

That day, as he wheeled about, the boy found a can of talcum powder. He opened it, mistaking it for icing sugar, and put some on his tongue. He spat it out several times, crossing the room in a hurry. Next to the crib, in a bright blue plastic case, he saw some sticks for cleaning ears. He tried stroking his fingers over them: they bent slightly, the two ends were covered with cotton wool so as not to hurt the inner parts of the ear. The boy took one and put it in his pocket. "Let's hope they don't notice," he thought. "Around it I can wind the thread I've found!"

With a single push of his feet against a wall, he crossed the whole room again. There was something on the mirror. He realized as he was passing beneath, raising his head for a moment. He went slowly back, moving the tips of his toes on the floor, like fins. Yes, there was something very high up, maybe a dirty mark, or a drop of dark liquid had been squirted there. He jumped onto the pouf but, just as he was stretching out to touch it, the spot suddenly came away from the mirror. The boy bent down to look at it, he felt it with his finger. It seemed like a tiny pellet. He took hold of it and squashed it. It was soft inside, almost liquid. He rubbed it again between his fingers and saw that it dissolved even further, expanded into a patch, all red. Then he realized it was a drop of blood congealed some time before. He paused again to look at it, on the tips of his fingers. And he wondered how it had managed to be squirted up there, and to cling there and remain attached to such a smooth surface, if the simple act of moving his hand toward it was enough to make it come unstuck.

The boy left the room and ran down to look at the thread, which was now dry. He snapped a piece off with his teeth and put it in his pocket. Later, on the bench, he showed it to the second granddad, who twisted it back and forth between his hands.

"I'll teach you a game!" he said at last.

He carefully knotted the ends together, put his hands inside the circle that it formed, and, by moving his fingers inside, began to form an intricate pattern.

"Now take it there, where it crosses. No . . . with just two fingers! Twist it around and take it carefully from underneath. You see? Now it's my turn."

The thread interwove differently each time, passing from hand to hand. It became more and more entwined, worked its way into the gaps between their fingers. Then the second granddad lightly touched the lattice with his long fingernail, at some crucial point, and the thread unraveled at once, under the astonished eyes of the boy.

"Oh . . . but how did you do that?"

"Watch, now we'll do it again."

He started to move his fingers once more. And while the horses were feeding with their muzzles in the sack and the thread kept constructing new patterns and then suddenly unraveling and interweaving and unraveling once again, endlessly, Abd rode ever closer, slipping through frontiers, secretly crossing the lands of the Franks and Lombards, his cloak flapping loudly in the wind.

Soon after, lying on the terra-cotta seat, the boy began winding the rest of the thread around the cotton swab. He held up a hand to shield his eyes from the chestnut husks but kept winding the thread around the stick all the same. The winding was never-ending. What an interminable job to transfer all the thread onto it, and to wind the large coils on the ground into such tiny coils! Not a sound came from the rest of the vegetable patch. The stick bulged more and more in the middle, and even the two wads of cotton wool had begun already to be covered. Meanwhile, Abd rode farther from Poitiers, covered in blood . . . Shortly before, entangled in the heap of bodies, upside down at some point toward the bottom, for a long while he thought he was dead. His feet must have been sticking out, he could feel a very thin slime trickle around his toes. There must have been a slight wind, a billowing air, made heavy by the heat of the flames, by the cries of the dying warriors, and by the distant shouts of the victors. Unless he was still on his feet . . . Maybe he was upright in a shallow bed of water, scorching from the sun, where tiny marine creatures were darting. And his head and his whole body were stuck into something that was bleeding heavily, maybe into a wound . . . For an infinity of time he thought he had stopped breathing. Finally, moving his toes against the sky, he began to suspect he was still alive somewhere.

He remembered nothing, by instinct he froze. He now managed to breathe among the tangle of corpses, perhaps it was through his feet that he absorbed the air. And it was certainly through his feet that he could also hear orders yelled from far away in a foreign tongue. There were skulls crushed against his own, a heap of rotten flesh that pressed against his teeth. He had to keep them clenched tight so that it didn't get into his mouth, dragging the whole heap behind it, but all the same he could feel something liquid seeping into his throat. "How did I end up here?" he wondered. There was a small space around his right hand. If he moved it, it finished inside a smashed skull. Yet more time passed. It had started to rain. His body suddenly began to return to life as if, through his feet, he were sucking some of the rain that was falling. Then, little by little, a cold air lifted, the rain stopped. Abd realized that, above the heap, night had now fallen. He rotated his ankles, flexed his long prehensile fingers in the darkness, and, in doing so, thought he had brushed against a helmet, felt it roll away rattling with the sentient head that was contained inside. If he wasn't really dead, he could try to slip out from there by opening a gap with what was left of his body. If he were stuck upside down, he would push himself out with his hands and arms, he would turn his chest even at the risk of causing the whole heap to collapse. And eventually, clinging to the top with hands and feet, he would pull his head out with a sudden thrust, hoping only that it wouldn't come loose from his shoulders. If, on the other hand, it was his feet that were lowest, immersed in the water turning ever colder in the night, he would have to push himself forward, moving his arms as if he were swimming, trying not to remain trapped by the mangled corpse of some warrior, or he could also get out by moving backward and maybe in the end he would find himself in some unknown place beneath the earth's crust.

He began to disentangle an arm, pushing against a head of wet matted hair, he tried to make his whole body vibrate, and a moment later a crash of metal, a creak of bones and of teeth suddenly rose from every side. There was also a groan from some distant part of the heap or of the night. Abd thought that maybe he had managed to move a little farther back, for he no longer felt the mass of flesh against his teeth. Unless his head, intent on making such conjectures, had now in fact detached itself from the rest of his body. He tried with all his might to twist what seemed to be his chest, hoping the heap would not collapse. He must have cleared a small amount of room. He moved back again. His lips were now pressing against the cold cornea of an open eye. He managed to move up a little farther still. But, however hard he tried, he couldn't figure out whether his left arm was still there. His whole face was squashed against another face, there was a kind of narrow gap he had to get through at all costs. He pulled his head back violently, and for a moment it seemed as though his hook nose was tearing the other face. A slightly larger space then opened up. He twisted his chest again to work his way loose, managed to bend his head before coming to a stop. His neck had come to rest on the razor-sharp blade of an ax. He moved back to the position he had started from and then, due to some subsidence inside the heap, he felt his body suddenly being thrust upward. He kept still for a while so that any new movement wouldn't squash him down to the bottom again. He wasn't sure where he was but seemed, after so long, to be breathing the distant odor of the night. His heart had begun to pulsate, making the whole heap throb. He moved back again, and not even the leg that blocked his path was a problem because, as he thrust it away with a violent movement of the hand, he realized no body was attached to it any longer.

When he found himself with his feet on top of the pile, stretching out against the distant glow of the flames, he realized that his body was wholly intact beneath the boundless night.

In front of the door, on a well-spread bedsheet, a pile of wool was building up, waiting to be carded. The mattresses had been torn open, one by one, by the wet nurse, who was now scratching about with her hand in the gash to remove the last great tufts of matted wool. From the ladder, the boy watched the pile growing, and the strange wooden machine that had appeared close by. When there was no longer anyone about, he got down to examine it more closely, its small seat, the handle and the drum, inside which, curved in opposite directions, lots of tiny nails stuck out all around without ever touching.

The pile continued to grow, was now as high as the door, and you had to walk around it to enter the house. From a first-floor window, the wet nurse was still throwing wool from pillows onto the pile, while the first granddad strolled in the vegetable patch with one of his nephews, an engineering student who had been staying for the past few days.

When the pile at last stopped growing and the wet nurse was away from the house, the boy went up to the first floor, closed his eyes, and, stretching his arms as far as he could, launched himself from the window.

A second later, he felt himself sink into the mountain. He remained there for a while, deep down, submerged in the wool, could hear the distant sound of the first granddad talking to his nephew and the shrieks of the wet nurse, who had started breast-feeding again. He was just about to fall asleep when someone took a large handful of wool near his head, then another, and yet another. A second later he felt himself grabbed by the hair. He gave a cry and struggled free, rolling out. There was a man sitting on the carding machine, pushing the drum back and forth nonstop. The boy picked up a tuft of wool already carded and carefully examined it: if he hadn't leapt from the mountain in such a hurry, his body would have ended up just as soft and weightless as this.

As time passed, next to the dense mountain, a new one began to rise up, smaller for the moment, but infinitely lighter. The man worked all day at the carding machine. When he went off, the new pile was higher than the old one, and reached up to the first-floor windows. After a long wait to make sure no one was about, the boy went up to the second floor, climbed on the ledge of the small window, and jumped.

That new pile was so soft that he seemed to dive into a cloud full of steam, felt his body drop into it like a stone, and for a moment he thought he would crash to the ground if the freshly carded wool hadn't stopped his fall just an inch before he landed.

He remained still, deep down in the pile, which had begun to swallow him up, raising its walls back up around him. He couldn't work out whether he was asleep or awake, slowly breathed the little air that managed to filter down there, and the only sounds from the vegetable patch and the house were distant and faint. If he didn't leave quickly, he thought, he'd soon be stitched up in a mattress along with the wool, and someone would lie down each night on top of him, and he'd have to shout at the top of his voice to make himself heard. The wind must have blown up. The mountain, absorbing the air, had cooled slightly, and he could breathe more easily. "I feel better now," the boy thought, deep down there. And he closed his eyes. A moment later, a horrifying muffled yelp came to his ears. He leapt from the pile, raced toward the road: Isabel lay in the center, with her rear paws completely torn off and bleeding.

That same evening, with the help of his nephew, the first granddad began drawing complicated designs on a sheet of paper. Next day, he shut himself up for a long while in his small workshop. When he finally came out, he was holding a wooden frame with two metal wheels at one end. He lay Isabel on the terra-cotta seat and tried to fix the frame to the rear of her body. He was talking intently with his nephew, they used words the boy had never heard before, waved their hands about now and then in the heat of the discussion as they tightened the straps with which they were attempting to fasten the back of Isabel's little body. But they didn't seem satisfied. They went back to the workshop, coming out much later: the frame had been much modified and seemed at last to fit around the animal's back as she lay on it anxiously, looking around, before attempting a few steps.

The first granddad and his nephew went off talking, toward the farthest parts of the vegetable patch. At lunchtime, while the wet nurse was serving at the table and Isabel's little wheels squeaked outside the door, the first granddad solemnly switched on the radio. But nothing could be heard, the words were mangled, came out disjointed. The first granddad banged it two or three times, loosened the screws with the point of a knife, took off the piece of hardboard that acted as a cover. A second later he was running toward the outhouse, still holding the open radio, shaking it furiously over the hole to get rid of a litter of mice that had nested in its tangle of wires.

His nephew left that same evening. As soon as he had turned the corner of the house, the boy went to the outhouse. In the light of two candles, one that he held in his hand and the other on the windowsill, now just a wick sailing on a drop of molten wax, he saw several whitish drops in the hole. "It must be wax," he thought, since he was holding the candle at quite an angle to see better. Just below, a large piece of excrement must have suddenly dropped onto the litter of mice. The boy put the candle onto the windowsill, squatted down to defecate. But only for a moment, because he jumped straight up with fear: he was scared that the mice, on seeing his little scrotum hanging over the hole, might grab hold of it as if on to a safety rope. He just urinated, from a distance, closing his eyes and holding the point of his penis, ready to stop in case the mice emerged from the hole in a long procession, one after the other along the stream of urine. Outside, the little dog was getting used to the frame on wheels, as the squeaking sound was becoming faster and continuous. The boy put out the candle and left the outhouse. He walked past the nettles with his hands in his pockets. They seemed to have grown even taller, were now as high as him. The big radio on the kitchen table was still open. The boy put his head inside to take a look: there was a mass of electric wires all nibbled, scraps of wood and filaments of freshly carded wool the adult mice must have carried inside to build their nest, passing through the hole for the wire to reach the plug.

Whimpering sounds were coming from the baby's room. Once he had reached his own room, the boy threw himself under the bedsheets, covering himself completely. In the silence, he could hear the squeaking of Isabel's wheels, practicing around the kitchen table. The baby on the first floor must have been sucking hard, for the whole house seemed to be continually wavering.

Next day, the boy got up before everyone else. He went straight down to the kitchen. Isabel was stretched out fast asleep on the floor by the table with the wheels in the air. The boy took a closer look. The pendulum clock made the wall of the room sway the opposite way. Suddenly, while he was still looking down at the ground, he heard a shriek from high up in the house. Isabel woke with a start and yelped, scratching the floor with her front paws, trying to turn the frame upright. The boy set it straight, then rushed up to the second floor. The cry had come from the wet nurse: sitting on the bed, she was biting her lips, pressing her breasts against each other. The baby, thrown to the far end of the blanket, was howling, swirling his legs and arms. His scrotum was so swollen with milk that it had hardly a wrinkle.

"Get out! Get out!" the nurse shouted when she saw him at the door.

Flying down the stairs, the boy was careful where he put his feet, so as not to roll down like a sack to the ground floor. He decided to climb the ladder and to remain up there all morning. The doctor arrived soon after. The wet nurse was feverish, crying out loud, a large mass of puss was accumulating in her breasts. "Mastitis . . ." the doctor explained to the first granddad, as he passed below the ladder. Isabel was yelping in the vegetable patch, trying to struggle free from the frame because she couldn't squat down to urinate. Just before lunch, at last, the sound of the whip could be heard from the road, and the furious rolling of wheels coming down the asphalt. The boy stuck his head out as far as he could between the two rungs, holding on tightly. Only then did he remember that on the day of Isabel's accident, while he was deep down in the heap of freshly carded wool, he had also heard a muffled noise, amid the confusion of other sounds, that could have been the crack of a whip coming from the road . . . He clung more tightly to the rungs, so as not to fall.

For some while there had been a quite a commotion in the outhouse. The boy climbed down quietly from the ladder and tried to get in through the door, but a hand held it firmly shut. "Don't come in!" came the voice of the first granddad, shouting from inside. The boy stood still, waiting. From outside he could hear the sound of water being poured onto the floor, as if the first granddad were frantically washing something. "Are you still there?" came the voice again, after a while, from inside. The boy kept silent. A few moments later, the first granddad came out of the outhouse. He was sweating, his face red, and he walked head down, dragging something in the dust. But when he looked up and saw the boy was still there, he gave a grunt of surprise and started hurrying toward the little workshop, hiding the large object with his body. The boy tried to move around him, but the first granddad carried on shouting to go away, throwing small kicks into the air. In this way he finally reached the workshop door. But in order to open it, he had to let go of that object with one hand . . . which he did. He lifted his arm toward the handle. In that same moment the boy saw an incredible animal dangling behind him.

The first granddad rushed into the workshop, closed the door with a bang. He emerged some time later, went quietly to his own room, and returned once more with a book. The boy ran to see what book was missing: it was the encyclopedia of animals. He came back down, jumped up to the first rung of the ladder and began climbing. "What had the first granddad found inside the hole?" he wondered. From what little he had seen, it looked like a large, unfamiliar beast, dead and drooping, colored here and there, enclosed maybe inside a large, heavily decorated turtle shell. Unless some ball of wool had become coiled inextricably inside the hole. It may have had a beak. It stuck out from a face almost black, wizened, and its legs and arms were hairy, with great long claws. Could it be a flying monkey? But how could it have found its way into the turtle shell? And how did it end up in the hole? Could it have grown up inside there? Maybe, from throwing in intestines and other animal remains, balls of wool and feces, drops of wax and soap bubbles, mice, snails, butterflies and eggshells, blood and everything else, a new unknown species had eventually formed, which the first granddad was trying to classify with the help of his encyclopedia.

But time went by and the workshop door stayed shut. The boy watched from a rung at the very top, swinging his legs slowly in the air. To keep his balance, he didn't even have to hold on with his hands. When he finally emerged from the workshop, the first granddad seemed greatly agitated. He locked the door and went off. He came back an hour later with two other men: the doctor and someone he didn't know who was carrying a folded bedsheet. All three went into the workshop and remained there for a good half hour. The boy listened, but couldn't make sense of their excited words. At last they came out. All three were holding the sheet rolled up, with that thing most certainly laid out inside. Walking slowly so as not to drop it, they went off, taking short paces, exchanging anxious looks, before disappearing round the corner of the house. All he could hear now was the sound of their cautious steps as they carried that thing who knows where.

The boy remained for another long while on the ladder, didn't climb down even to eat. Little by little he began to suspect . . . His feet swung faster in the air, and in time his body leaned forward, so that he was barely sitting on the rung. He clung on with his hands. His heart began to race, because he knew just a moment earlier he had almost fallen. He suddenly realized what that thing was.

"Abd!" he exclaimed, shaking his head beyond the last rung of the ladder.

And he didn't even notice Isabel, who began barking all of a sudden in the middle of the vegetable patch. He saw that dark, shriveled head again, that beak, which was none other than his large wizened nose, his legs and arms onto which were attached all the hair and feathers accumulated over time inside the hole, the great turtle shell that had just happened to swallow him up or in which he had become trapped, who knows when, while he was coming up or going down for the umpteenth time to the center of the earth.

Isabel was still barking in the middle of the vegetable patch. The boy roused himself, jumped down in a few leaps from the ladder. He ran as fast as he could to the second granddad's villa, running so fast that, for the first time, without realizing it, he went right into the garden along the path. The second granddad was leaving at that very moment. He was strolling along the path with a white suit and light walking stick, and waved his straw hat to greet him.

They walked a long way that day, until almost supper

time. It was now very hot, and the boy was wearing only sandals and a scanty pair of colored briefs, alongside the second granddad, who was fully dressed. They talked excitedly. The boy recounted everything that had happened, the second granddad waved his hat to fan himself, moving it quickly against the sun.

When they got back to the boy's house the second granddad went into the outhouse because he had to use the toilet. He remained in there for a long time as Isabel rushed about in the vegetable patch, making her wheels squeak. "I haven't oiled them for a while . . ." the boy thought as he crouched on the ground outside the door. Once the second granddad had come out of the outhouse and gone off toward the villa, he ran inside and lit the candle. He also lit the wick on the windowsill, still fixed in a tiny drop of wax, for one last time. He hesitated long before looking. When at last he lowered the candle over the hole and knelt to the ground with his head bent, he realized straightaway that the second granddad was about to die.

He stood up and trembled slightly, his sharp shoulder blades nudged against the wall. He closed the hole with the lid but first, with the help of a stick, he pushed down one of Isabel's paws, which was jutting out. The wet nurse must have thrown it in after the accident. A firefly, passing the open window, came a little way into the outhouse, paused for a moment, and then, perhaps on seeing the two lighted candles, went back out. The boy left the outhouse and crossed the whole vegetable patch, head bent. Silently he passed the Signora, who, with a long dress down to her feet despite the heat, was walking along a tiny path. He called Isabel, who hurried squeaking toward him. He oiled the wheels of the frame, and the little dog ran off again. She stopped, then carried on running even faster to see whether the squeak really had gone. The boy watched the increasingly voluminous body that wobbled on the frame. A few days earlier he had asked the wet nurse why. She had carefully examined the animal. "She's pregnant!" she said at last. "She's expecting puppies!"

The boy lay on the terra-cotta bench, covering his eyes with his hand. The wet nurse's screams were coming from the second floor. The doctor was with her, lancing her breasts to drain the puss.

Now, in the great heat, the hole was churning. The boy often ran to pour buckets of water into it, afraid that its contents, swelling further and further from the depths of the earth, might rise into the air like a great wall. Beside it, there was now a stick: it was used for stirring about inside, for pushing down the bulkier objects, for poking a network of holes into the thick crust of feces so that the water could seep through. The wet nurse, in particular, used it when she had to throw bundles full of puss into the hole. "There must be a blockage somewhere . . ." the first granddad said. "We'll have to call someone."

Perched on one of the top rungs of the ladder, the boy was waiting for the arrival of the man who had to remove the blockages, when, looking up, he saw the Signora standing still in the vegetable patch. It was the early hours of the afternoon, and the air seemed almost on fire. The Signora, standing at an angle, was staring sideways at the boy's body. The dress at the base of her back suddenly rose and, due to the angle, it looked like the spine of a centaur lopped off cleanly with a saw. She was looking straight toward him. The boy began to wriggle his little bare body on the ladder, creeping from one rung to the other, until the Signora raised her arm and, without a word, summoned him with a slow, repeated hand movement. One rung after another, taking care that his briefs didn't drop down too far as he moved, the boy started to climb down the ladder. Once he was on the ground, he stood still for a while, as if standing at attention. The Signora summoned him again. Then, moving his little legs slowly over the ground, he finally reached her. He was now standing right in front of her, and she remained at an angle. She stared at him, seemed to want to erase him altogether from the vegetable patch.

"He's dead!" she said finally.

The boy realized she was talking about the second granddad, and lowered his head.

"It happened yesterday evening . . ." she added. "They called me in the middle of the night to dress him!"

The boy went off, after he had walked around her large

dress to reach the path. Passing in front of the nettles, he stopped for a moment, face-to-face with the last large, threatening leaves. They nodded slowly at each breath of wind, bowing as if to sneer. The Signora meanwhile strolled off, her dress swishing across the grass. From the house, there was not the slightest sound. The boy went to the outhouse and shut himself inside so that no one could see him.

Much later he heard a discreet knock at the door. Standing flat against the wall, he decided not to open. He heard another knock. He didn't move. But a few moments later, looking up, he saw that the space of the little window was filled by the face of a smiling man. He was looking at him silently. Who knows how long he had been there. The boy opened the door and ran to climb onto the ladder. Meanwhile, the first granddad emerged from the house. He greeted the man and went with him into the outhouse. They were talking, but the boy couldn't work out what they said. Then the man came out of the outhouse, went to the edge of the vegetable patch, and stripped completely naked. His gigantic body moved very slowly, as if in water. His great feet held the ground in a vise. The boy looked round and saw the wet nurse leaning out of a second-floor window with her breasts bandaged. The man picked up an unblocking device with a lance that he had propped against the wall, walked all the way round the vegetable patch, and eventually stopped in front of a stone from which a large rusty ring protruded. The Signora was watching him too, standing still in the distance. The man took hold of the ring, gave it a force-ful tug, still holding his lance, and lifted the stone high into the air. Then he let it drop with a thud, and the boy thought the whole vegetable patch was about to fall apart. The man studied the passage that had been opened up, his giant body crouched for a moment on his heels. He frowned, swung the lance he was holding, then jumped down into the hole. The first granddad leaned over the gap, trying to look inside while the man shouted back in answer to his questions. There must have been a passageway down there because the man's cries were moving, and the first granddad hurried through the vegetable patch banging the heel of his shoe on the ground every now and then. The man gave a shout from below to signal where he was.

He was underground for more than an hour, continu-ally moving about, shouting more and more, as if preparing to engage in some great battle. Then there was an extraor-dinary silence, and the boy felt as though an imperceptible vibration were shaking the vegetable patch and the house and the section of ladder on which he perched, as if the man had thrust his lance into the throat of a gigantic mon-ster that was now flailing about in some place deep down in the earth. More time went by. Then a soft sound that shifted here and there through the vegetable patch indicated that the man was singing happily underground.

A few moments later the point of the lance began to appear from the opening to the passage, then the black head of the man, then his whole gigantic body, like a statue of mud and ink.

The man rolled the stone over the hole, moved toward the house, to the square of concrete in front of the door. His feet left perfect tracks on the ground. He looked up toward the ladder, and the whiteness of a smile appeared for a moment on his black face. He stood still, in the middle of the concrete, removed the hosepipe from the nail, uncoiled it, opened the faucet, and, as the water glided over him, that black, fetid crust slowly fell away from his body, like a second skin. The lines of his face began to struggle free behind the veil of water, his toes moved on the concrete, continually changing color. Then, having picked up a piece of soap, he began to rub it over his body. His swift hands produced a thick lather, from which tiny bubbles of soap blew off. After he had rinsed himself once more with the hose, he got rid of the patch of filth on the concrete, washed the soles of his feet again, dried himself, dressed, combed his hair, and walked away from the house, whistling, with the lance over his shoulder.

The wet nurse then came down from the second floor, went into the outhouse with the stump of a broom and a handful of detergent powder. When she came out, the boy went into the outhouse too. He opened the door and jumped inside. But he immediately stopped: resting on the circle of the hole, a single enormous bubble almost entirely filled the room.

The boy moved very slowly back, went and stood still against a corner. He stayed staring at the bubble in disbelief. Could it have come out of the hole by itself? Or had it been caused by the wet nurse's detergent powder and that constant pouring of buckets of water into the hole? The boy pressed the bones of his body as far as he could against the corner of the room, trying not to breathe for fear that his breath might be enough to burst that great bubble. He didn't urinate so as not to pop it. Slowly he closed the window, for he knew the legs of a fly or some other tiny insect would burst it straightaway. Meanwhile, the bubble swayed slightly over the hole, its perfect sphere somewhat distorted. It seemed about to take off, and the boy waited for it to rise up at any moment like an air balloon, and for a small colored gondola to appear from the depths of the hole with tiny hands and claws that waved from its edges in sign of greeting.

Tired of standing, the boy crouched on his heels, making sure that his pointed knees wouldn't touch the bubble. On its convex surface, he saw his own fleeting image.

When he finally left the outhouse, opening the door very slowly and then closing it again with a thousand precautions, the bubble was still there. The vegetable patch was empty, apart from the great nettles that nodded their heads, whispering to each other. Every now and then, half opening the door and peering through the crack, the boy checked whether the bubble was still there. It began to get dark.

Much later, he went in to check. He pressed himself

against the wall but could see nothing. Without leaning forward, he crept along the wall to the window, stretched his arm as far as the candle stub and the box of matches. He paused for a moment, held his breath, then lit the candle.

The great bubble appeared at once. The flame of the candle reflected on its surface next to his face in deep concentration, and the light whirled in every direction around the gleaming sphere, created vortexes suspended by centrifugal force, pinwheels in which different-colored lights formed, like tiny moving windows, and the boy kept turning his head to try to see inside, following the orbits that glanced off the sphere, pouring down like a cascade of light into the hole.

It lasted just a few moments. The great bubble then broke. And all at once the hole, closed off so long by that great pocket of air, began suddenly to talk.

The boy rushed out of the outhouse, not even putting down the candle. By the time he realized it, he was already at the far end of the vegetable patch. He stopped and looked around before deciding to return. He blew out the candle, pushed open the little window pane from outside, and put it back in its place.

The first granddad, returning home much later, went into the outhouse. "Yes, now it's flowing well!" the boy heard him murmur soon after. The baby on the second floor had begun to cry. The wet nurse rinsed out the milk boiler before going to him. The boy went up to his room. He took off his tiny briefs and hung them carefully on the tip of the nail.

In the silence, despite the distance, he could hear the hole still murmuring to itself in the heat of the night. Its voice rose from time to time, or fell into a sullen silence, muttered something, and then, immediately after, gave out a furious, shrill cry, as though someone had contradicted it. It went silent for a while, then continued whispering very slowly, incessantly, and it seemed as though something were plunging without further hindrance into a great hissing whirl.

The boy listened for a long while. When he felt he was falling asleep, he pulled the little ring that protruded from the polystyrene head, and the music at once began to play, gradually covering the other voice. Meanwhile, sitting on a ridge, Abd imagined a Bedouin tent at an immense distance. He didn't know exactly where it was. He knew only that he had continually pressed ahead, that he had crossed countless frontiers. That he had killed and slaughtered, robbed, and burned, dug up dead bodies to plunder them. That populations, different each time, had gone after him before he disappeared once more in some new city, staggering in his cloak along swarming streets. That he had run through crowds of men and beasts, that he had watched from the window of an inn while a smith was busy shoeing a stranger's horse, until the hammer went missing and the horse and the horseman and the smith had gone missing too, as well as the sound of hammer on iron, with not a nail left in the emptiness of the street, in front of the sign for the little workshop swinging in the air.

A group of soldiers was heading up toward the mountain in the darkness. Abd could see the shadow of their hooked javelins in the distance, could hear the sound of padded mechanical footsteps in the night air. He had known for some time that a Lombard duke was after him. His mind was lodged in a vague point of space, and he felt gripped by an obscure nostalgia. He held his tongue a little way out, with its tip he could feel the sounds that vibrated in the air. And by sticking it out a little farther he could go even as far as touching the indescribable joy of minds that plowed the night armed to the teeth, like glass marbles. He stuck it even farther out, to the extreme cavities of darkness, felt it project its infinite lines far into the distance. "Maybe one day," he thought, "some wayfarer, on lifting his torch deep in the night, might see the signs traced by my tongue in space. At least this will remain, at least this incontrovertible eternity will remain!"

The sound of marching footsteps was now drawing close. Abd saw once again the floating shadow of the javelins, a battle axe silhouetted against a glow of stars. Seated on a rock, Abd waited. His great hook nose concealed the moon.

The hole kept on talking for a whole day, protesting ever deeper down. The boy passed back and forth near the outhouse, walked toward the vegetable patch, lay down in some place not far from the stone, from where the echo of a constant murmuring rose up. He went into the outhouse, removed the lid and knelt on the floor, putting his ear close to listen.

And again, all the following night, the hole continued talking. In the darkness of the room, the boy listened intently, drying his sweat with the bedsheet. He kept waking and going back to sleep, until a deafening sound woke him with a start. He jumped down from the bed and ran to open the window. He was not mistaken: the hole was singing loudly in the silence of the night, the sound came from somewhere deep down in the earth, where the section had perhaps caused a last blockage to explode with the buildup of its weight and was now plummeting down into a vast thunderous cavity.

Peering from the window, the boy leaned out farther into the night, as into a soft slime. Straining his ear, trying in vain to catch the words of the song, which seemed to disappear now and then, leaving behind it an immense sound with a steady rhythm, like the panting of breath in a vast hollow space. The night air was sweltering. The boy stayed at the window for a long while, until his little legs began to buckle with fatigue. Then he went back to bed and fell straight to sleep, with not enough time even to cover himself with the sheet.

He was woken by a ray of light that came in through a gap in the shutters. He put on the little briefs that hung from the nail, went down into the kitchen, then to the vegetable patch. Isabel rushed blindly back and forth, in an apparent fit of delight. Her wheels had begun to squeak again. As she came up to him, the boy loosened the straps of the frame as her body had grown even larger. At that moment, the wet nurse came out of the house, heading for the outhouse with a small bag. The Signora was already walking about at the far end of the vegetable patch. The boy climbed up the ladder and stayed there listening for a while. The crack of the third granddad's whip hadn't been heard for many days, he had disappeared once again. The doctor arrived soon after. From high up, the boy could see his nodding head, which seemed half asleep, while a thousand sharp objects jingled in his large case. Moving noiselessly around the vegetable patch, the Signora bent down every now and then to sprinkle salt on the snails. The first granddad was going off to work with a book under his arm. There were small piles of salt here and there in the grass, where snails were bursting out of their shells, and it was hard to tell whether it was the snails that were absorbing the salt or the salt that was drawing the snails out of themselves.

The boy began moving about, one rung after another, on the ladder. Screams were coming from the second floor. They were cutting the wet nurse's breasts. The squeak of Isabel's wheels suddenly stopped in the middle of the vegetable patch. The boy closed his eyes, rested his shoulder blades against the wall of the house, and remained in this position for some while. A long time later he heard drowsy, muffled footsteps beneath the ladder. He climbed down and began slowly to cross the vegetable patch. Passing close to the great nettles, he closed his eyes for an instant to concentrate as much as he could. He wiped the sweat from his brow and from his little chest, brushing a hand over his ribs. Close to the terra-cotta couch Isabel was whining and twisting her head in every direction and seemed to be suffering. He went up to her and saw a long thread sticking out from her throat. She must have found the little stick for cleaning ears that he had hidden in a secret place at the foot of the couch, and she was still swallowing the thread, always hoping it was about to finish. Every so often she stopped, tried to vomit, contracting her whole body. Stroke by stroke, the boy began to pull it out very gently, since it must already have gone deep down into the esophagus and maybe even to the stomach, had maybe already reached the most intimate parts of her body, where her puppies were forming. There was indeed a steamy froth around the thread, and Isabel stared at him amazed, holding her mouth patiently open.

When he had extracted everything, the boy went back into the house: it was deserted. The first granddad was now at the truck scale, and the wet nurse, after her medication, must have gone out shopping. The baby was sleeping naked in his room on the second floor, with no sheets because of the heat. On the pillow was some milk he had puked up, right next to his mouth. The boy lay on the padded pouf on wheels. Only his feet were sticking out, and his head, which dangled over the floor and was turning dark because of the blood. He remained like that for a long while, then his legs began to move, pedaling softly over the floor-boards. He moved across the floor, his head studied every object intently. A stove and gas bottle were in the middle of the room, there since the wet nurse had stopped breast feeding, and several white cloths ironed and stacked, and a basin he hadn't seen before.

The baby moaned slightly in his sleep, turned an arm and moved his face into the puked-up milk. The boy started moving around the room again. He rolled slowly in ever smaller circles. He was no longer looking around and therefore let his head hang down until it skimmed the floor. He came to a sudden halt, held his arms around the circumference of the pouf, gripped it with his hands so that it wouldn't slip away. Then, pedaling once more, he hurtled across the room at great speed, back and forth several times, braking hard just before he smashed his head against the wall, causing the wheels of the pouf to rise off the floor. The whole house shook, the floorboards seemed about to give way, and several objects fell down from the wardrobe, which was struck several times by the edges of the pouf as it careered out of control, and crashed on the floor. The baby, woken by the noise, cried out, writhing in the crib like a small animal. The boy's body collided against the walls and the corners of the furniture, the pouf hurtled about the room ever more ruinously, until it overturned.

Still clinging to its edges, the boy felt his skull crack while the whole of that great mass rolled over him like around a pivot. The baby's cries had now become convulsive. The boy, lying on the floor, pressed the bones of his head. He lay there for some time, not opening his eyes, fearing he had gone blind. At last he got up, took a few steps across the room, went up to the crib. He stared at the puckered face of the baby, who was crying uncontrollably, his eyes shut. He studied him for a long while from close up. The baby's eyes had now suddenly opened, must have sensed the shadow of a face suspended in the air above him. The boy leaned over the crib, paused for a moment, as though balancing.

Then he put his lips on the open lips of the baby, who stopped crying straightaway.

In the house there was now a great silence. The baby's tiny head relaxed little by little, was already breathing calmly in his sleep. Without making a sound, the boy left the room and went down to walk for a while in the vegetable patch. He climbed up the ladder, down a few rungs, then back up. He watched his small feet moving, spanning the gaps between one rung and another. There was something that puzzled him. He couldn't work out whether the rungs were getting farther or closer apart. "To find out I'd have to climb up it in the middle of the night," he told himself after a while. The vegetable patch was deserted. The legs of the first granddad's table had sunk a little farther into the ground. The boy stood listening, but no cracks of a whip came from the road. "Who knows where she's got to?" he wondered. He was thinking of Isabel. He went down two rungs and stopped. Climbed three rungs again. Sitting on the top, he dangled his legs for a while. He went back down and jumped to the ground. He crossed part of the vegetable patch and arrived in front of the large nettle leaves. They were face-to-face and stared each other in the eyes. For some time he thought the hole was quietly calling him. He looked around, went into the outhouse. He lit the candle, letting a few drops of wax drip onto the edge of the hole so that it would stay upright. He removed the lid and put his ear very close. Kneeling on the floor, he frowned a little as he strained to listen. He moved his ear even closer, bracing himself with his hands, until the expression on his face suddenly seemed to change. He seemed not even to be breathing. He held his mouth half open and nodded every now and then in agreement.

He remained perfectly still for a long while, the flame of the candle lit his face in deepest concentration.

"Yes, mama," he answered at last, softly.

He lifted his head from the hole, very gently replaced the lid.

Then blew out the candle.

Clandestinity

1

He turned the handle to get into the house, pushing the door with his shoulder at the same time.

"I don't remember locking it . . ." he thought, banging it harder.

But the door seemed stuck.

He waited a moment before throwing his whole body against it and immediately felt an imperceptible, elastic movement, as though someone on the other side were trying with all their strength to keep the door shut.

So he stopped, took a few steps back, and looked around. By the door, on the ledge of the window onto the landing, there were two empty flower vases and behind, against the grimy window pane, a barometer in the form of a statuette, a dancer holding up her tiny skirt, which, given the color, showed bad weather on the way.

"But this isn't my house!" he suddenly realized.

He hurried back down the stairs. "I must have climbed an extra floor without noticing . . ." he thought, hardly looking at the steps. Why hadn't he realized immediately, when the door failed to open at the first push? The person on the other side must have been there against the door at exactly the same moment he was trying to open it. Maybe he had just arrived home or was preparing to leave at that very moment . . . or maybe he'd taken a step back and had his shoulder against the door, and in front of him there was someone moving forward step by step. Or her . . . why not?

This was why he had felt the whole door give slightly. A great number of tense muscles must have been straining and pressing from all directions, like a bone. And he even thought he felt for a moment the body of the other person against his own body, as if the door itself had wriggled free under the pressure of two opposing forces, reproducing on a single plane the form of two bodies in combat.

Soon after, back home, he opened his shopping bag, washed a piece of lung at the kitchen sink, rubbing his hands over its spongy surface, pushing his fingers into the opening of the tubes to let the water in. He put the piece of lung into the pressure cooker, then washed a dish and some cutlery as he waited, looking out of the window, setting the table.

"It's been whistling now for ten minutes," he said to himself, opening the valve to let out the steam.

He took off the lid.

Beneath him, in the pan, the lung released another great quantity of steam.

He pricked it with a fork to see if it was cooked.

At that very instant it struck him full in the face.

"It's burst!" he said to himself, not saying a word. "It was that piece of lung! It's burst in my face!"

Boiling water and scraps of flesh kept coming free from the deflated lung, as if thrown out from a bomb. At the very moment of the explosion there had been a sound like a distant blast just as the outer membrane of the lung, saturated with boiling water in every pore, was being pierced by the fork. Something was murmuring beneath him, gave out a wounded sigh inside the pan.

He ran off shrieking, afraid he had been blinded.

He bathed his eyes at the washbasin in the bathroom: they were red and peered at him in the mirror like the eyes of an animal struck in the face. Water dripped from the kitchen ceiling, and pieces of lung dropped down. A very large scrap of flesh lay splattered over the floor, steaming and quivering.

It was waiting as always at the top of the staircase. A long tumor swung with each step beneath its stomach, almost brushing the floor.

Dragging its load with much difficulty, the cat walked the stretch of corridor that separated it from its own doorway. It started meowing.

"It wants to come in . . . it gets worked up when it sees my shopping bag," he thought, giving it a stern look.

Not mean but stern, to keep a distance.

"It was better when they used to bandage it all up," he thought.

Until not so long ago, an old lady who lived on the same landing used to wrap its body with gauze from its rear to its front legs.

He quickly searched for his house keys and opened a narrow crack in the door so the animal couldn't get in. Some day or other, he thought, that creature would end up attacking him. He could only hope its bulge would prevent it from getting off the ground, from leaping up. In that case he could always defend himself by kicking, striking its head with his boot before it went for his legs . . . Unless it managed to spring up all the same, spring up from the ground and attack him in the face, jumping into the air with that thing . . .

There was a musty smell in the house. He opened the window of its one room. He went to look at himself in the mirror: his face was scalded in several places, especially around the lips and eyebrows, he felt it burning. The garbage bag in the kitchen area still contained pieces of torn, burst lung. He decided to throw it down the garbage chute on the landing. He opened the door, catching sight of the cat. He thought maybe he could throw it a piece of lung.

"Impossible!" he thought. "Then I'd never be rid of it!"

He hurried to the garbage chute, opened the hatch,

dropped down the bag, and returned inside, all before the animal had time to notice, to pick itself up and make its way meowing toward his door. He inspected the walls of the kitchen area: they were marked here and there, up to the ceiling, and around the edges of each patch were fragments of lung that now looked like mold. He shut the window, switched on the small light by the bed, and turned off the main one in the middle of the room. He went up to the small portable television, bent down to switch it on in the semidarkness, not noticing the pointed aerial that was sticking out. He froze, his eye a few inches away. He turned it round toward the wall, just to be sure, then switched on the television.

He sat on the edge of the bed to watch: some butterflies were sucking the excrement of a chimpanzee, a gorilla of vast proportions had a comb made of bone on the top of its head and a hippopotamus was marking its territory with dung. The male that could throw it farthest won the highest position in the group. It spread it with its tail and sometimes ate it. Fish fed on the plankton produced from the fermentation of hippopotamus excrement. The Lombards. The monasteries on Mount Athos. During the commercials there was some music he seemed to have heard somewhere before, many years ago. He felt a thrill of excitement. "No one can see me, no one will ever know a thing about any of this," he thought. Two hands started playing the piano on the floor above. They had been practicing just over his head for a year now, always at the same hour, and the sound could only be coming from the apartment he had tried to get into by mistake the previous day. And so it could have been those same hands that had kept the door so firmly shut . . . or maybe other hands, hands that were imprisoning the hands that were playing the piano . . .

A water pipe started to make a noise caused by a pocket of air. He got up and opened the faucets in the kitchen and toilet. The noises and the vibrations abated slightly, then returned.

He switched off the television and lay on the bed. The hands upstairs continued playing. He tried picturing them: they were large hands, with loose skin especially round the thumb and index finger to allow the hands to stretch as far as possible, hands able to strangle . . . or perhaps they were small and white, bony, always on the move, autonomous, complete with their own heart, brain, digestive system . . . He imagined coming into contact with those hands: that he was going to the floor above and the door this time was open, as though someone were actually waiting for him, but the picture wasn't clear, nor was it clear whose hands they were. At a certain point he imagined them around his penis, masturbating him while he was asleep.

He was thinking that the hands of someone who works on dissected bodies were white and cold, always in contact with frozen meat and refrigerators. They seemed made of another substance, there was something that went through them and it was impossible to work out where the hands ended and the dissected bodies began. Did the hands end where the dissected piece ended or was it the dissected piece that began where the hands began?

The hands of the woman who sold rabbit, pheasant, partridge, and grouse were just like that: white and cold. Around her nails there was always a trace of blood and tiny scraps of flesh that looked like jam. He had watched the woman many times. He'd been misled at first by her tall hairdo that looked like flax, and the heavy makeup around her eyes. He had decided she was crazy. But as time went by, due to a whole series of factors, he realized she was wearing a large wig, that her eyebrows were drawn with a pencil, and that her eyelashes, so long and heavy, were certainly false. It was obvious: some strange illness had caused the hair to drop from her whole body. So he couldn't help thinking that her sex must also be bald and hairless in the same way, that her hands, in their incessant movement through the day and night, must go back and forth who knows how many times between her bald sex and the butchered animals, constantly transferring bits of their flesh countless times to the gate of her vagina and vice versa.

There again it was enough to interpret the landmarks that appeared on the surfaces of food. And to decipher hands.

The dairyman's were dark, hairy, they gave the impression of being rather boneless as they covered the freshly cut cheese with greaseproof paper or layers of thin plastic. He kept a piece of white meat, pork, always in the same place, which he sold in slices. All around were containers of milk and other foods, almost liquid, watery, with sticky white surfaces that left traces on the long blades of the knives. The dairyman's wife came down to the shop an hour later and she too began touching the surfaces of the food with the tips of her fingers, so the four hands would sometimes be operating together, one pair next to the other behind the glass of the refrigerated counter, a sonata for four hands. He studied those fingertips in the early hours of the morning. He couldn't work out why, but the dairyman's left hand, the one with the wedding ring, gave him the impression of having slept all night deep in the woman's sex. And nothing ever completely disappeared, he thought, people could wash as much as they wished but there's always something left behind, in one way or another, merging with other substances and other bodies, weaving storylines, new genetic probabilities. He half closed his eyes and saw filaments teeming everywhere, frantic little beings with heads and tails, spermatozoa.

Once back home after shopping, he often found himself having to decipher the surfaces of food. He sometimes came across a hair curled up in a fetal position inside the hole of a slice of Emmental, or traces of pink, extremely pale, perhaps the last residues of menstrual blood heavily diluted. They were sometimes so cold that he could remove them with his fingernail. Or he discovered minuscule strands of hair of such a strange color as to hint at the idea of adultery. When the circumstances came together and he found a suspicious strand of colored hair next to a trace of pink, he could suppose he had discovered an adultery committed while the woman had been menstruating to avert the risk of fertility.

Another day had gone by. Having overcome the cat's siege unscathed, he went inside. He laid the table, opened the shopping bag, put a slice of gorgonzola on the plate, switched on the TV and began to eat. The mold and the green patches on the slice of cheese created a composition in whose filigree, that day, he could read nothing. But the arrangement of the dots, of the filaments and of the crevices, the sudden grouping of dark patches in a single place, in some form of skirmish, conjured the image of a battle. They were all attacking someone.

On the TV screen, a man was reviewing a pile of recently published books on an arts program. He opened one of them, cleared his throat before starting to read:

Xenophon recounts: "Cyrus's six hundred scatter in the rush to pursue the troops as they take flight, and very few men, intimate friends and table companions, are left around Cyrus. While he is with them, suddenly he sees the king not far away, surrounded by his chief advisers; he doesn't waste a moment and on shouting 'There he is!' he rushes at him, strikes him in the chest and wounds him through his breastplate: this was reported by the physician Ctesias, who treated him soon after. While Cyrus is wounding the king, a Persian soldier delivers him a heavy blow beneath the eye with a javelin. Ctesias states that many Persians were killed in this clash between the soldiers of Cyrus and Artaxerxes. But Cyrus himself is killed, and on top of him fall eight noble followers. In this regard, the accounts refer to Artapates, the most faithful of his followers. He sees Cyrus mortally wounded and leaps from his horse to cover his body; but it is not clear whether the king has him slain upon the body of Cyrus or whether he kills himself with his own dagger, of solid gold."

He was still staring at the piece of cheese on the plate. "Yes of course! That's exactly it!" he suddenly thought. That dark point with a small crevice was none other than the king, and the other one next to it with what looks like a lance, that was Cyrus . . . The fighting was clear, and to one side the eight faithful followers heaped on Cyrus's corpse. And those clear, whitish marks, speeding all around, they have to be the manes of the horses, the tufts of hair rushing about on the ends of lances and the tops of helmets.

On returning home he saw the front gate covered with funeral drapes.

A tall lectern decked out with black satin had been set up by the mail boxes. On it was a large open book.

As he went by, he could see several signatures in neat lines on the first page.

He took the lift. When he opened the wire mesh door to get out, he saw the cat crouching immobile in front of him. It wasn't meowing, was perfectly calm. There were several people on the landing, right in front of the old lady's door, which was covered with purple, black, and whitish drapes, faded and shaped in pointed folds. Those drapes and the heavy structure that held them seemed out of place on the dingy landing. "They fix those things up with no thought, no consideration even for where they are," he told himself.

He opened his door and went inside.

After a while he thought he heard the sound of footsteps on the landing. Strange . . . he'd heard the old lady coughing only the previous night. He sat on the bed for a long while, with his legs under the blankets and his head and back against the wall, doing nothing. And all of a sudden he heard several faint coughs coming from the other side of the wall, then one of those cries he had happened to hear at other times, maybe some exclamation, part of a word spoken aloud in the middle of some animated conversation the old lady was having with herself, one of those cries or shrieks that might slip out in a moment of excitement when someone is accustomed to living alone.

He rubbed some cream over his eyelids and around

his mouth and tightened the faucets since the water pipes were rattling and vibrating, louder and softer, from different places, like musical notes held as long as possible. But there was no improvement. So he tried opening one of the faucets, just enough for a trickle of water to come out. This strategy had worked at other times, causing the noises to stop straightaway. This time, no. "The combinations are obviously continually changing," he thought. So he opened the faucet fully. This time the noise stopped, but that sound of water gushing so violently was just as unbearable as the rattling of the pipes.

He switched on the TV: they were transmitting a foreign language course. He stopped to listen for a while. Then he fixed a triangular wooden floor block that was continually coming loose. He hammered down the nail so it wouldn't stick out. He often walked around with no shoes and had already once caught his foot on that nail, tearing the heel of his sock.

He opened the window to let in some air. He didn't feel like eating, whatever came to mind seemed entirely inappropriate.

All the same, he made the effort to cook something. He set the table, trying not to forget anything so as not to have to get up while he was eating. At the beginning of meals, it was always difficult to get food into his stomach. It wasn't just a foreign body. It was a hostile body, there perhaps against its own will. Inevitably. But a body which, once propelled into the corridor of the esophagus, into the black sack of the stomach, had still to find its way out, at the risk of tormenting, tearing away a part of the body, dragging everything with it. For this reason he had to start little by little, with tiny mouthfuls, carefully studying their reaction, as if to set a trap . . . But once tempted in, it was difficult to get rid of it at the other end. It stayed inside him for a long while, transforming and accumulating, but, contrary to all expectations, caused him no inconvenience, it seemed as though it wasn't there, he felt not the slightest need to expel it. He succeeded in defecating only at the station. He went into the main halls, walked along the interminable succession of platforms and after a while felt a violent need to evacuate. He emptied himself completely in the lavatory, unimagined apertures suddenly opened, which erupted vastly and endlessly and, being closed up inside there, seemed to him to express a tiny notion of the infinite.

But if he went to the station for that specific purpose, nothing happened.

With much patience and diplomacy he nevertheless managed to eat something, even if he hadn't reached that brief moment of peace and exhilaration that sometimes seized him at the end of the meal. He wanted only to go out. He looked outside: it was already dark. The building opposite, with dozens of illuminated windows, seemed to be lit from within, as if there were neither doors nor windows nor stairways inside.

He went out. On the landing there were still several people at the old lady's door, neither inside nor out, half hidden by the drapes. He couldn't work out whether they were standing there out of a sense of respect or because the room was now overcrowded. He couldn't hear a sound.

He went down by the stairs. On the floor below he passed two middle-aged women who were coming out of the hairdresser's. Under their crimped hair, stiff with lacquer, their faces looked forbidding. He passed the open door of the hairdresser, who worked until late in the one-room salon beneath him. He caught sight of a woman under an old-fashioned hair dryer and the outline of the girl who washed hair in the back room. Over a gas meter, next to a pile of boxes of dye, was a polystyrene head of a woman that might once have held a wig. He saw it each time he went down by the stairs, immobile behind the grimy window looking onto the landing.

In the corner of his eye, as he turned onto the next flight of stairs, he saw that the girl was carefully watching through the gap in the door.

He arrived in the street. He took several side roads, walked alongside the railroad embankment. After a while he noticed a woman was walking fifty yards ahead. Time passed and neither of them changed direction. The woman turned round a couple of times, pretending to look to one side. He began to walk, making as little noise as possible so as not to frighten her. But at the same time he realized this silence, for her, might suggest he was creeping up behind her. He tried to quicken his step to overtake her, but the woman, on hearing his footsteps closing in, began to hurry, nervously. There again, he couldn't walk slowly: the woman would think he was trying to hold back so as to attack her after she had turned the corner of the block. He tried crossing the road: by moving onto the other sidewalk he would show a clear intention to take a different route. But the woman must have thought he had done so only to catch a glimpse of her face before attacking her . . . When he crossed the road once again, the woman stopped against the wall: she had her legs tight together at her knees, her feet apart, doubled up with her hand on her belly as though she had a stomach pain.

He stopped. She was panting but was looking at him meanwhile with a wild confidence.

"She's like me! She's like me!" he suddenly thought.

The woman put her hand on his wrist, taking hold of it for support. In that moment he felt extremely weak, his legs would no longer support him. He rested against the wall with his hands and with a cheek, and slid down.

The woman stopped to study him for an instant. Then shouted. She started to run, continually shouting for a hundred yards or so, before she entered a house, and her shouts could still be heard, more faintly due to the distance, though they had multiplied.

Having overcome that first moment of exhaustion, he too began to run, yelling loudly in order to keep going, and as he passed the house the woman had entered, a brick narrowly missed his head, landing on the ground and breaking into two large pieces, each of which, if it had hit him, could have smashed his skull.

Walking past the large open book on the lectern, he could see that two pages were now covered entirely with signatures: some small and neat, others scrawled, which merged at various points with nearby signatures, others that meandered around the other signatures as though searching for space without ever touching them, yet others sharp and irregular, contorted and pointed, all inextricably jumbled together.

He went past without signing. As he went up in the lift he could see from above that the concierge had come out of her room and was approaching the book on the stand, no doubt to check whether he had decided at last to add his own signature, the only one missing.

The cat was still there, in front of the lift, but once again it didn't meow and didn't run up to meet him. It was squatting on the floor and gave him no more than a hard stare. Its long swelling lay on the ground and, among the others, looked like a limp fifth paw.

He opened his door. At that same instant the water pipes started to clank, almost as if on purpose. He opened the window and switched on the television. Then, in the bathroom, he washed his hands, face, and armpits.

Once he had washed, he felt he wanted to go out again, even though he had only just returned. He went onto the landing. At the old lady's door, which was still open, no one was there. He tried to move closer to look inside: the old lady was laid out in the middle of the room, but not in a casket nor on the bed, maybe on a chest of drawers or a large trunk hidden by sheets and pillows. Two female figures were bent over her, level with her stomach. They suddenly looked up. One of them was in front, shielding the corpse. The other, half hidden, stopped busying herself around the stomach, then hurriedly covered it again. She seemed intent on arranging the corpse's underwear as best she could, on making certain checks. He wasn't sure, but he thought the woman was trying to hide something in her hand: the end of some nondescript object was jutting from her fist.

It only lasted a few seconds. Then the two women moved toward him. One of them asked: "What do you want?"

He wasn't sure he had properly understood the question because, at that very moment, a burglar alarm went off in the street. He noted something in the woman's expression that resembled the old lady's features. Perhaps she was the daughter.

He shook his head.

"Nothing," he replied.

He realized someone else was in the room, someone he hadn't noticed until then. Something very bright moved in the farthest corner. It looked like the white coat the dairyman wore in the shop. But he couldn't be sure. The person was standing in the darkest part of the room, and his face could hardly be seen, his white coat seemed to float in the shadows, suspended alone, three feet from the floor. And yet that person turned toward him, stood there motionless, making no attempt to hide himself, as if, by standing still and fixing him straight in the eye, he would gradually become invisible.

He went down to the street, walked for an hour, but when he found himself back outside the house he had no recollection of what he'd been thinking the whole time he'd been away.

He went back inside. He walked past the large book again. This time the concierge was outside her room. She had stationed herself close to the stand with the excuse of flicking dust from the mail boxes. When she saw him, she stopped dusting and gave him a harsh look. She seemed to want to say: "This is your last chance!"

He walked past without signing, went up in the lift, into his house, opened the window, switched on the television. A moment later the water pipes started going. As well as the usual sounds, there was a violent shudder, like the hammering of a machine gun.

He tried tightening the faucets but with no success. He opened one of them, the usual one, making one of the sounds even more shrill, almost a whistle. So he decided to open it fully. But that strategy also proved pointless. It produced, indeed, another noise, at regular intervals, resembling systematic sniper fire. He tried alternately opening and closing other faucets but, after an initial pause each new combination just produced the same result, changing it only slightly, as though someone were stepping in each time he intervened. As though everyone were opening and closing faucets, calculating the pockets and blockages of air with a perfect understanding of the state of the pipes throughout the building, as though they were transmitting to each other the latest procedures for attack in that new metropolitan language.

"These are words!" he thought. "They're signaling to each other!" They were talking about him, had their own codes, their own charts fixed to the wall, and were operating on the faucets like on the keyboard of the most sophisticated teletypewriter. They could work out every language, introduce emergency languages in any situation, produce variations, intervene on other soundtracks. He could tighten all the faucets he wished, they were capable of neutralizing the aggression of his silence. They were talking among themselves, and he understood nothing of what they were saying.

He then tried playing his last remaining card. He opened all the faucets in the bathroom and the kitchen, flushing the toilet too.

Every other sound stopped. There was a moment of uncertainty at first, a few noises lingered, reemerged in other sounds. Then nothing more, only the splash of flowing water that poured out from every part. "What's going on now in those homes of theirs?" he thought. "Tonight the building really will have no walls or doors, no stairways . . ."

He went to bed without eating. But he couldn't sleep. The splash of water was enormous, never-ending. All of a sudden he thought he wouldn't survive a minute longer, that it was all over. Then a moment of unconsciousness came. He was lying on the edge of an enormous waterfall. The noise rose to maximum, then it fell. He felt from a moment that he was sleeping deep down in that primordial silence.

The morning began with shuffling sounds on the stairs and the landing, so much whispering that it seemed to come from a multitude.

He had turned off all the faucets and, despite this, there was no noise from the pipes. From a gap in the shutters he could see the funeral director's hearse and several people around it talking quietly among themselves. The back door of the hearse was open.

He heard anxious voices on the landing. He moved toward the door and realized they were having difficulty carrying the casket down the stairs. Someone had suggested they use the lift. He heard the clatter of the lift door being opened with too much force, the noise of something knocking and banging. They were discussing how to get the casket into the lift, which was narrow. The agitation grew, a dozen voices intermingled just outside his door. The landing didn't seem large enough to contain them.

"Let's hope they find an answer soon," he told himself. Otherwise someone, sooner or later, would end up looking distractedly at his door, would inevitably come up with some idea, would have a word or two with those others who were busily trying to find some way of getting the casket into the lift. And they'd then break down the door using the casket as a battering ram, and once inside his apartment in that intemperate state, there's no knowing what would happen . . .

He placed his ear against the door. He managed to work out that those outside, after various unsuccessful attempts, had come to the conclusion that the only way of getting the casket in the lift was to stand it upright in the cabin. But since the door was low, they had to begin by taking it in flat, then raising it more and more to one side as it gradually entered. "The old lady certainly can't keep still in that position, inside there," he thought. She'll end up in a huddle, and those outside would be bound to hear her as she moved. And the outline of the casket against the mirror of the lift would appear, to anyone who happened to see it as they passed on the landing, like the back view of someone busily checking themselves in the mirror during the short journey to the ground floor . . . He had sometimes happened to see them in that position, glued to the mirror, with their neck and head rigid and terribly twisted, so absorbed that they hadn't noticed the lift had already arrived at its destination and that someone had opened the door and was getting in . . .

The lift moved off, the landing gradually emptied itself of voices. He hurried to look through a gap in the shutter. The casket arrived after a few minutes. They slid it into the hearse, which left straightaway. It turned its nose into the flow of vehicles traveling in the opposite direction, created a small gap behind it, where those taking part in the funeral procession could be safe.

The cortege had gone barely a hundred yards before a burglar alarm went off and the water pipes also began to groan and fire off the first warning shots.

"This is the moment!" he thought. "There's not a minute to lose!"

He opened the wardrobe and the drawers, filled a suitcase and a small rucksack with clothes, and cautiously left the house. He called the lift. The cat stared at him without meowing, immobile. But it suddenly lifted itself onto its four paws and seemed to be concentrating all its bodily energies to the full.

The lift arrived straightaway. He dived inside. He feared the cat would throw itself against the cabin to attack him as soon as he had started going down, sinking its claws into him, even at the risk of it being torn apart in the narrow gap between the floors.

But it didn't move.

The concierge wasn't there on the ground floor. "She'll have gone to the funeral too!" he thought. All the same, to be safe, he didn't leave by the front door. He crossed the yard and climbed over the railing in one corner after he'd thrown the suitcase to the other side.

He went to the car, which was parked a hundred yards away. He hadn't used it for months and felt sure it wouldn't start.

He threw the rucksack and suitcase inside and turned the ignition. Surprisingly, it started the first time.

The seats in the station waiting room were almost all occupied by people stretched out asleep. He found an empty place and sat down. At the other end of the seat, a large dog was sleeping. He tried to shift it, but it felt as heavy as lead.

He was exhausted. He lay down on the seat, stretched out, resting his head against the dog, which didn't move an inch. He was comfortable like that, with his cheek against the fur of the animal's stomach, and fell asleep inhaling that infinitely good smell.

2

"Now I'll open my eyes!" he thought.

He was still lying on the bench and was taking up its whole length. Under his neck there must have been a newspaper folded to act as a pillow. But he seemed to remember his head had been resting on something much more comfortable at the time he'd gone to sleep.

"It must have been resting on someone who had to go," he thought, "and was kind enough to put this newspaper underneath before leaving."

He yawned, opening his eyes.

By the bench, a man was staring at him.

He immediately sat up.

"What are you doing here?" the man asked.

He was standing over him, motionless, and was smiling.

"I must have a temperature . . ."

The waiting room was almost empty. Many must have gone off during the night, by train.

"What are you doing here?" the man asked again. "Don't you have a home?"

"I don't think I can go back."

The man bent slightly over the bench, still smiling.

"Yes, yes . . . but how did you end up here?"

The man remained silent, waiting for his answer.

He wiped a hand over his forehead, dried the sweat.

"I saw you by chance walking along the corridor," the man continued. "I almost didn't recognize you. It's been quite some time!"

He looked at him without saying a word, and made a gesture with his hand.

"Okay, okay, you really don't want to tell me!" the man observed, exposing his teeth in a brief smile.

Meanwhile, he put his legs down from the bench, tied his shoelaces. He felt slightly unsteady. He stood up but fell back immediately onto the bench.

"You can stop at my place for a while, if you wish," the man said as he helped him up. "I'm living somewhere else now. Just give me the time to take my stuff away . . ."

He paused, waiting for an answer.

"You can come today, before evening," he continued. "I'll leave the key under the doormat."

Soon after, once the man had gone, he headed slowly toward the platforms. He started walking back and forth on one of them, among travelers waiting to depart. Then he left the station, moving slowly away. There were puddles of water in the streets, caused by blocked drains that hadn't managed to carry away all the rain that had fallen during the night. There were planks here and there so that pedestrians could cross certain flooded patches without getting wet.

He walked for a long while in no particular direction, waiting for evening to come. He was moving farther and farther from the center, through unfamiliar areas almost deserted. Suddenly he remembered his suitcase and rucksack were still at the station. He had left them at the checkroom shortly before going to sleep on the bench in the waiting room.

"I'd better go back to collect them," he thought.

So he changed direction and returned to the center. Passing in front of the restaurants, he gazed through the large windows, peered at the faces of people busily eating behind the glass panes. When they saw they were being watched as they ate, they stared back angrily. He must have walked a long way, he thought he would never get back. "And then I have to find that place," he thought, checking the address the man had written down on a piece of paper. Gradually, as time passed, lights appeared in more and more buildings along the streets, on the signs, in the puddles of water where the lights were reflected for a moment before being canceled out by vehicles, by their wheels, as they drove past.

"This city isn't here," he thought. And meanwhile he felt tears welling in his eyes.

Once inside, having locked the door, he put the suitcase and rucksack on one of the two beds and began an immediate inspection of the small apartment inch by inch.

In the kitchen there was a dish on the floor under the sink: it was full of chicken innards and cockscombs, probably food for a cat. In the bedroom were two beds, side by side, one already made up and the other with just the mattress on

its frame. At the far end of the room was the empty frame
of a crib. He opened the wardrobe, pulled out all the drawers: they were empty. He bent down to look under one of
the beds, then the other. There was something under one of
them, at the far end. He stretched his hand out and seemed
to touch something damp and cold. He drew back immediately. He took a toothbrush from his rucksack and used it to
slide the object slowly out from beneath the bed. It took him
some time to figure it out: it was a piece of cotton wool with
a speck of blood. It must have been down there for quite a
while, in fact it was no longer white but gray, almost black,
due to the dust that had gathered. He opened the drawers
of the nightstands by the beds and in one of them, passing
a finger over the paper that lined the bottom, he thought he
felt something. With a coin he pulled up the drawing pin
that held down the paper and was immediately confronted
by an obscene image. The photograph was not very clear
due to the extreme closeness of the lens to the object being
photographed, but he seemed to think it was an open vagina
and anal sphincter, into which had been placed numerous
objects that formed a kind of irregular radial pattern. He recognized a ballpoint pen, a knitting needle, a pen and a hen's
neck, a toothbrush, several pieces of uncooked pasta, and a
frayed piece of lighting cord.

He returned the picture to its place and fixed back the
drawing pin. He went into the bathroom. There was a mirror
over the washbasin. Moving closer until he almost touched

it, he checked his face: the scald marks were slowly healing. Inside the bathtub, like a children's game, was a long meandering caravan of letters of the alphabet, made of plastic, each different in color, all laid out in single file and heading unknowingly toward the plug hole. They were led by a strutting purple-colored capital P.

"A child must have been living here too, in here," he thought.

He gathered up the letters and put them in a box, emptied the dish of chicken giblets into the garbage bin, and went back to the bedroom. He took a chair, moved it to the wardrobe, and climbed onto it to look up there too. In doing so he realized that behind the wardrobe was a door, made of thin wood, locked and covered by a sheet of Christmas paper. He tried to open it using the key he had found under the doormat, but it didn't work. He pushed the wardrobe away from the door and bent down to look through the keyhole: he could see nothing. He tried sticking the lead of a pencil into the hole and saw that it went through, indicating there was no obstruction. If he couldn't see the other side, it meant it was dark in there, or perhaps something had been placed intentionally over the handle, a towel or some clothing.

He pushed the wardrobe back against the door and went to open the window. Opposite, close by, the back of a building obstructed his view of anything else. He continued looking around: he found a transistor radio, some binoculars, and a TV, which he tried switching on. It worked. He left it on and went to the kitchen to look for something to eat. He found nothing. In the refrigerator there was just a piece of yellowed cheese, a half-empty jar of coffee, several boxes of pills, and two batteries. He licked his finger and put it in the jar of coffee, then sucked the powder that had stuck to it. It had an unpleasant taste. He spat it into the sink. The apartment seemed to have been unoccupied for some time, which was why he couldn't explain the dish of chicken giblets which had been put there recently and suggested there was a cat, which there wasn't. He shut the window again, searched in the refrigerator for some pills that might be of use. He found something against influenza, swallowed two tablets with some water, and went to bed fully dressed.

When he woke he was soaked in sweat. Outside it was dark. He needed to get up to find something to eat. He went out in silence, not even switching on the stair lights, and went down to the street. He asked at the bar nearby, they pointed him to a small door next to a shop with its shutters down. He went there and walked in. Once inside, there was a staircase in front of him. He climbed two flights and found another door. He opened it and found himself in a tidy apartment. People were crowded in front of a piece of furniture on which he could see a slicing machine, some small scales, and, to one side, a music box. A woman was slicing some cured meat, while other members of the family were sitting eating nearby in the kitchen. "It must be where the owner of the shop on the ground floor lives," he thought. "She must carry on selling in her apartment on weekends when the shop is closed."

The woman at the meat-slicer seemed rather anxious, kept an eye on the people around the furniture, especially the customers' children, who were running here and there, touching everything, and were dragging each other across the room in a large cardboard box.

His turn came. Once he was near he could see several sheets of newspaper and a piece of oilcloth had been laid under the slicing machine so as not to mess the surface of the furniture. The woman kept pushing a piece of meat against a revolving blade, passing so close with her fingers, and he couldn't work out whether it was for this, or because she chewed them, that her fingernails were reduced to sore and jagged stubs, with raw flesh, cut and swollen, around those minuscule remnants.

He returned to the apartment. As he opened the door he had a strange feeling he would find it occupied by a Black man sitting on a throne. A magnificent throne, decorated with brightly colored designs and tufts of white hair, so large as to occupy half of the bedroom and so tall as to raise the man's Black head to the ceiling.

He went in. The apartment was empty. He made an effort to eat something, then swallowed two more tablets and looked outside. He could see a dim halo of light in a window of the building opposite, no doubt the light of a television switched on in a darkened room. The television, though he couldn't see it, must have been against the wall to the left of the window. But he could see a woman sitting on a long couch, directly opposite, and something close to her that was moving. He took the binoculars, turned off the light so he could watch without being seen. The object moving by the woman was a hand, which kept changing in size and sometimes looked large, sometimes very small, sometimes formed by a small hand on top of a large hand, like in a process of instant expansion. In all probability it was a child sitting on the knees of an adult, busily playing at touching his father's large hand with his own. Nothing else could be seen. But the whole of the woman was visible: she was bent slightly forward and had her hands between her knees, which knocked together from time to time.

He put down the binoculars and hurriedly switched on the television: he wanted to find out what they were watching at that exact moment in the house opposite. But it was difficult to work out. He changed channels several times. He paused for rather longer on one of them, attracted by the music and the succession of images: inside a seventeenth-century house, in a large hall, a number of women seen from behind were watching a man intent on playing the piano in a far corner. Their small heads were fixed on top of enormous billowing dresses.

He went back to the window. It was still just the same as before. The changes of brightness in the window opposite matched the alternation of images on his television tuned to that last channel. "That's what they're watching," he told himself. He began to get ready for bed. When he returned to the window to lower the shutter he noticed straightaway that the scene in the house opposite had changed. He pointed his binoculars and saw that the woman was now lying back on the couch and the large hand and the small hand were no longer there. She lay still, on her side. Through his binoculars he had a perfect view of her neck, which in that position seemed very broad, and the tip of her chin. He took a closer look at her face and, once accustomed to the light and its variations, he realized the woman wasn't asleep at all, that her eyes were open and, without knowing it, she was looking toward him.

He remained there for quite a while, studying the body that lay there pretending to be asleep. All of a sudden he saw she was moving. There was a hand, a large hand, resting on her waist: it shook her as if to wake her. He quickly focused on her face. He saw her eyes were now shut. Some time passed. Another hand was placed on the woman's hip, this time the small one, which began to shake her more firmly, thinking she was asleep. The woman kept her eyes perfectly shut. Then the large hand took one of her bare feet and shook it several times, the small hand took the other foot. By shaking her, the two hands had parted her legs, and her skirt had risen to her groin. The woman was now on her back, her head lodged in the corner of the couch, and at that contorted angle her neck had become even broader. He looked at her face through the binoculars and saw that the woman, pretending to wake up, had opened her mouth, perhaps to simulate a yawn. But the image he perceived was the hideous expression of someone who had been hanged.

The woman finally got up from the couch, the TV was turned off, and nothing else could be seen.

He lowered the shutter, turned off the light, then the TV, undressed, and went to bed. He was restless, he felt a rancid taste in his mouth. The presence of empty furniture in the darkness made him anxious. He got up, switched the light back on, divided up the pile of clothes on the floor, and managed to put something into each drawer and even into the wardrobe: trousers, underpants, socks, which could occupy two separate drawers, singlet, shirt, jersey, handkerchief. At the end he realized two small drawers of the wardrobe were still empty. He undid his shoes and put one shoelace into each of them. He went to urinate in the kitchen sink. To make quite sure that no one would hear him, he pressed his penis against one of its marble sides so that the urine would come out slowly and perfectly silently. Once he had finished, he opened the faucet for just a moment so that the flow of water would wash away any remaining traces. Then he went back to bed. But soon after he remembered he hadn't checked which way the door that was hiding behind the wardrobe opened. He dropped off to sleep for a few moments and woke again. "I'll check tomorrow," he thought. He was shivering with cold. He curled up at the bottom of the bed, but there was so little air down there that it was hard to breathe. He had to keep his head out, he stretched a hand across and felt the bed beside him for the first time. He searched for the light switch because he couldn't recall how the room was arranged. From what he remembered about the layout of the furniture and the walls, he thought the headboard of the bed was against the wardrobe that concealed the door. He switched on the light and everything returned to its proper place. He went back to sleep only to wake up again: he was talking aloud in his sleep. A noise started to come through one of the walls of the room. It sounded like the voice of a woman pleading with someone over and again. Another voice interrupted her every now and then. The first voice suddenly grew louder, seemed to want to prevent something terrible. She kept on endlessly repeating a phrase that was always the same, which he couldn't figure out. That person was certainly crying. Then the voice stopped coming out with words and phrases, was transformed into an interminable, tortured moan, but one that more and more resembled the uncontrollable sounds of an orgasm.

He sat up on the bed. He didn't know what to do, those sounds were getting more unbearable, they seemed to be coming from a dismembered body. He distinctly heard her crying again.

He fell asleep and woke again a dozen times, and each time, once awake, he heard those sounds that faded and then returned. The last time he looked at the clock on the night-stand he saw he'd been in bed for many hours. He reckoned now that someone on the other side of the wall was intent on torturing someone else to obtain continual orgasms with manual equipment or by using some small machinery with its independent and relentless motor, holding their face deep between the wide-open legs of the other to gain a bet-ter view of their sex now in full agony.

He managed at last to get to sleep. The noises on the other side of the wall had become more intense, terrifying. Just before falling into a deep sleep he thought he heard a new sound coming this time from the other side, from behind the wardrobe: it was as if someone were making a circular rubbing movement with the sole of a shoe or a sheet of newspaper against the floor.

Next morning he woke late. He got out of bed and went to the window to raise the shutter. He'd only just taken hold of the pulley strap when he realized he was wearing no under-pants. He went to the bed to put them on but couldn't find them. On the floor there was just a pair of shoes with no laces. Then, so as not to remain naked as he pulled up the shutter, he took hold of a sock that was sticking out of the half-open drawer of a nightstand and slipped his penis into it. He pushed the sack of his testicles inside too, so the sock wouldn't fall off. He could feel the light pressure of the elas-tic around the base of his genitals as he went back to the

window. The long, dark covering that hung between his legs
tilted slightly forward, throbbing. He realized his penis was
filling the sock that he could now feel all around it, apart
from the tip, which had become hardened with sweat, where
his toes had been. He began to pull up the shutter and, in the
few seconds it took him to do so, his penis had become erect,
completely hardening the sock, which was now fairly tight,
even if the bulge of the heel caused it all to distort slightly
to one side. When the shutter was fully up, he looked outside. At that same moment the half-lowered shutter of the
apartment opposite slowly went up, and behind it was the
woman he had seen the previous evening pretending to be
asleep on the couch. He felt certain straightaway, as soon as
he saw her, that she'd been watching him through the tiny
holes between the slats of her own half-lowered shutter: she
stared at him, her face almost against the glass. He remained
stock-still for another few moments, while the sock continued to wave about by itself. Then he moved away from
the window, searched again for his underpants, but they
really weren't there, nor his other clothes. Only then did
he remember that during the night he had scattered them
around in the drawers. He opened them one by one. He
slipped on his underpants, his trousers too, and went back
to the window. There was nothing apart from the usual window of the building opposite, but the shutter next to it went
up a little way, enough for him to see, a few moments later, a
patch of hair that stood out against something very light. He

lowered his shutter a little way and, pointing the binoculars from a dark corner far away from the window, he realized it was a woman's sex between two white legs splayed apart. He couldn't see the head of the person, which was hidden by the shutter, but it was clear the woman was sitting on a large packing box and that there must have been something inside it, given that it could hold the weight of a person. He tried to read the name printed on the box but could make out only two large letters at the end, an A and a Y. It must have been a storeroom piled with boxes and other objects that could be glimpsed vaguely in the background. The patch of hair, given its relative proximity and the strength of the binoculars, looked enormous in the large circle that framed the image. A moment later he saw a hand that moved up to the sex holding a long dangling object, blue in color. A finger began to introduce the long flimsy thing, gradually pushing it inside until all that could be seen was a small ring, slightly darker in color. The object had disappeared almost miraculously, swallowed up by the woman's body. He saw nothing else for a while, then a hand moved a brightly colored cylindrical object toward the sex, inserted the nozzle at the end of this cylinder into the small blue ring that was sticking out from the vagina. The first hand gripped the cylinder more firmly, the second began a rhythmic movement and seemed to be pumping, because another small cylinder inside the first was continually moving in and out of the larger one. "It's a toy pump!" he suddenly realized. While the hands kept on with this continual movement, the woman's body bent farther and farther back, lying gradually down on the box, and he could now catch a glimpse of her stomach, though slightly in shadow, and something broad and white, probably her neck, that emerged between two equally white masses, which must have been her breasts. Once she had stopped pumping, the two hands removed the cylinder, and, pulling the ring sticking out from the vagina, they made a complicated movement, as if to knot something. With the utmost care, while her legs splayed farther apart, they began to extract a voluminous blue object from her vagina, which grew even larger as it gradually emerged, moving gently each time that it suddenly broadened, followed by an equally sudden reduction. To extract the final part, the hands had on several occasions to tilt the large, bright blue mass that had just appeared: it was an enormous protuberance that stuck out almost by itself from a large balloon and must have resembled the large, stylized beak of a duck.

The balloon, which the woman held by its knot with two fingers, remained dangling in front of the crack of her vagina, between her open legs, and it seemed impossible to him that something so enormous and so flimsy, which seemed almost larger than the woman's own waist, could have been blown up and expanded inside that small opening, spreading then into her whole body before slowly emerging, with no apparent effort, without tearing and bursting.

A moment later the gap of window through which he had seen all of this suddenly closed, and the shutter beside it also dropped down precipitously and with a great thud, as if the pulley strap had broken.

He went back to the bed and finished dressing. As he put his socks on, he felt some moisture at the bottom around his toes. He opened his suitcase and distributed his clothing among the drawers and the wardrobe. As he flattened a rolled-up singlet, he heard the sound of something falling to the floor: it was his old slingshot with its forked metal handle. He then remembered he hadn't checked the door behind the wardrobe. He pushed the wardrobe, keeping it steady with one hand so that it wouldn't topple over, and saw immediately that the door had no hinges on his side: which meant it opened into the other room, or whatever that blackness was that could be seen through the keyhole. So the wardrobe wasn't actually stopping anything and, once the door was open, could easily be pushed to one side by sliding it over the floor to enter his room.

He pushed the wardrobe back against the door and, looking out, saw a shutter had been pulled up again on the building opposite, not that of the storeroom, nor that of the room with the couch, but another, the kitchen. The woman was walking around the room holding a plate and putting a piece of food into her mouth every now and then with a fork. She suddenly moved to the window and, still holding the plate with one hand and continuing to eat, she looked him straight in the face for quite a while. He too moved closer to the window, to look at her. After the woman had moved from the window and disappeared again, he remembered he still had some food from last night. He tried to eat too. But, once he had finished, he vomited everything into the toilet bowl. He swallowed two tablets and put the pill bottle back in the refrigerator. He got into bed with his clothes on. He had no intention of sleeping, just wanted to lie there waiting for the tablets to take effect. Then he'd go out shopping.

A couple of hours later he got up. He drank a lot to make up for the liquid he had lost sweating. He found it difficult to stand, felt as if something enormous was about to shatter at any moment inside his body.

He dressed but, out on the landing, the sight of the stairs made him feel dizzy. Looking round, he saw a young woman was staring at him at the doorway next to his. She was wearing a bathrobe which she held with one hand across her stomach, though it was tied with a belt. He nodded at her, she made no response, continued staring at him, saying nothing, studying him. And even after he had turned onto the stairs he could feel the woman's eyes staring behind him as he walked down unsteadily.

The air in the street seemed to revive him, he managed to walk without difficulty, not even aware of his legs and all of his body as it moved slowly along the road, as though weightless. He turned into a tunnel that went under the railroad tracks. Walking along the narrow sidewalk on one side, in the roar of engines and heavy air impregnated with exhaust fumes, he felt even lighter and bodiless, as if the sound waves that stratified and intersected in the tunnel had formed a pneumatic cushion that supported him, exerting a relentless and involuntary movement of legs and arms.

After the tunnel, he passed a restaurant that took up the whole corner of a block. Behind the curtains he could see a geometric succession of small moving heads. At the far end of the room, through the open door of a wood oven, the fire glowed unmistakably.

A little farther on, he went into a store to do his shopping. At the end of the block, he turned the corner into another tunnel. Soon after, opening the door of the apartment, he had the feeling that someone had been inside during his absence. He gave a quick look around to check there was no one hiding. He didn't want to lock the door and find himself face-to-face with another person in a house from which there was then no escape. When he was sure he was alone, he quietly shut the door and began a closer investigation. He immediately noted several tiny details: the blanket on the bed was too taut, as if it had been lifted and then pulled up too far, and there were several small differences in the way his clothing was arranged in the drawers. The slingshot, which was lying on the nightstand with the elastic well coiled around its metal handle, had certainly been touched. The leather pouch had been turned over: this meant that someone had unrolled the elastic and then rewound it without noticing the difference. Who could it have been? Maybe his host had had to drop by to collect something. But, in that case, why go and fiddle with the blanket on the bed, why had he turned up exactly during that brief absence, and lastly why, on finding he wasn't there, didn't he leave a note telling him he had been by?

He checked the bed more closely, lifted the blankets, and when he was quite sure there was nothing hidden inside, climbed in, fully clothed. He remained there lost in thought for a long while as darkness fell. When he got up he realized it was almost suppertime. He went to the window: in the building opposite all the lights were on, and behind the usual window, in the room lit up in front of him, there was a new, awkward presence. He knew what it was even before pointing the binoculars: the bright blue duck-shaped balloon was in the middle of the room, it bounced up against the ceiling from a punch that someone must have given it a moment before. The woman was carrying plates and cutlery into the room, while the child was amusing himself by taking hold of the thread of the balloon, which came down to his height, and tugging it. A man in a sweatshirt suddenly appeared, switched on the TV, then moved almost completely out of his field of vision. He was no doubt sitting in the same place as the previous evening, given that he could still see a hand and part of the forearm. The child ran toward the man and partly disappeared. He reappeared soon after. He moved under the balloon and, taking hold of the thread that hung down from above, he gave it a firm pull. He started hitting it sideways with his head, knocking it up and catching it in the air, hugging and kicking and punching it, biting it and rubbing his lips over it, wetting it with his saliva, pinching it, rubbing his fingers over it to make noises from it. Then he took it to the man, who rested his whole face against it. He could see him now and then as he and the child punched and headed the ball and rubbed their fingers over it. The woman, who was continually moving between the kitchen and the room, watched the scene for a moment before staring into the darkness, toward him.

Soon after, at suppertime, he could see the balloon above the table, still up against the ceiling. It swayed from time to time when someone inadvertently brushed against the thread with their hand or arm as they stretched across to pick up the salt pot, or a bottle.

He switched on the light and began eating too, sitting on the bed with his back against the headboard and the plate on the nightstand. He had almost finished when he heard the same noise he had heard the previous night, from behind the wardrobe: it seemed once again as if someone were rubbing the sole of a shoe or a sheet of newspaper against the floor. An instant later he saw a white shadow dart, quick as a flash, across the room. He jumped out of bed: on the floor was a small piece of paper folded in two. Someone must have slipped it under the door behind the wardrobe, calculating it so perfectly as to send it that far with the careful flick of a finger, like a glass marble.

Before picking up the note, he gave the wardrobe a heavy kick. The creak of the wood as it took the blow, and the loud echo, left him shaken. He listened for a moment, but no sound came from the other side. He bent down, picked up the piece of paper, opened it, and read:

> Go tell him this; and add,
> That, if he overhold his price so much,
> We'll none of him; but let him, like an engine
> Not portable, lie under this report —
> Bring action hither, this cannot go to war:
> A stirring dwarf we do allowance give
> Before a sleeping giant: Tell him so.

He started pacing across the room, unable to stop for a moment. Then he rushed to the apartment door. The landing was deserted. He went back inside, moved the wardrobe to look through the keyhole of the door behind it. There was no sign of light. He remained perfectly still for a while, with his ear and his whole body against the door in the hope of catching even the slightest evidence that might betray the presence of someone on the other side. But there was complete silence: a silence so complete, he thought, that only the presence of a living person could produce it.

He moved away from the door and absentmindedly

punched it. He froze once again. But there was still no sound from the other side. He glanced at his hand and saw that his knuckles were bleeding slightly and the skin had come away in two places. The Christmas paper, fixed to the door with drawing pins, was now also torn at one point, and a comet star dangled in midair.

He pushed the wardrobe back against the door and began pacing across the room again. He was shivering, or rather his body was shaking uncontrollably. But at the same time he felt his strength was slowly beginning to return. He switched on the television, ate some more as he paced about. The room was suddenly full of music, as a voice commented on various reconstructions of the city of Nineveh: hanging gardens overlooked the water, winged bulls, the king accompanied by the guard as he poured sacrificial oil over captured lions, several wild asses shot by hunters' arrows and attacked by dogs, a man in the act of strangling a lion, great terraced marble buildings and men and animals on the banks of the Tigris, long boats with their bow and stern raised like dragons or serpents and sails and long rows of oars that reflected in the water of the river. In the middle of the boats tiny canopies under which sat even smaller, solitary figures, and finally the clay tablets with the cuneiform writing of King Assurbanipal recounting the epic of Gilgamesh, two-thirds god and one-third man, who defeated Humbaba, the fierce guardian of the Cedar Forest, whose roar was a storm and whose mouth was fire, who dared to call Ishtar, goddess of love, a whore, who beat the celestial bull, saw his friend Enkidu die, and, having crossed the ocean of death, finally encountered Utnapishtim, who opened the small harbor mouth on the seventh day and saw some light fall on his face, while the human race became all earth . . .

His shivers had turned into a continual tremble, his eyes could see nothing for the tears. He gave out short, muted cries to hold back a pent-up mass of air inside him. Flailing his arms, he struck the bare light bulb that hung from the ceiling, smashing it into a thousand pieces. He felt its fragments caught up in his hair, in his eyebrows. He left the apartment, headed toward the neighbor's door, rang the bell, and, when she came to open it with her usual bathrobe and hands across her stomach, he stood speechless, immobile, tense, in front of her. After the first moments of surprise, she shook her head uncertainly and ran a hand two or three times through her hair before fully opening the door.

"Come in! You were right to come!" she said, while he suddenly realized where he was and felt he had nothing to say, didn't know why he was there, had completely forgotten what to do in situations such as these.

"Don't stand there at the door, come in!" the woman continued. "Aren't you the one who's staying next door?"

And she put a hand on his arm, gently pulling him inside.

He went through a small entrance lobby and into a very tidy room. There was a narrow double bed, a table half laid.

On it, a plate with several chicken bones, a ball of bread, and some orange peel. On the unlaid half was a television, though tuned to a different channel, showing cartoons.

He made another gesture to leave.

"I'm not sure why I'm here . . ."

She shook her head and disappeared into the next room. Meanwhile, seeing that he couldn't go just like that, he sat down.

"I'm sorry," she said as she returned, "I can only offer you a yogurt."

And she gently poured the contents of a bowl into a strainer resting on a much larger cup. She began to stir it with a spoon and finally, looking at the tiny heap of milk culture left in the strainer, observed: "It just never stops growing . . ."

She weighed it in the strainer, waggled her finger in it, and, before returning it to the other room, added: "I'll leave it hungry for a while!"

When she came back, he had already swallowed several spoonfuls of yogurt. The woman saw he was trembling.

"Eat what you can," she said. "I'll have what's left."

Then, watching him as he leaned forward, she noticed he had several fragments of glass in his hair.

She gave a look of alarm.

"But there's some glass in your hair!"

She took a thin nightgown that hung over the back of one of the two chairs, spread it across her knees, made him bend his head over it. She began to pass her hand through his hair, and pieces of glass, some fairly large, others very fine, almost invisible, began to rain down onto the nightgown, and even when they had stopped falling she kept on, to make sure, passing her hand slowly through his hair. She picked up the nightgown, folding the edges together so as not to let them drop, and carried it into the bathroom. As she shook it over the toilet bowl, from the other room he could hear the tinkle of small pieces of glass hitting the glaze before falling into the water.

"I'll go now," he said, when he saw her return.

He moved toward the door. She opened it.

"Come back whenever you like!" she said, before gently shutting it again.

He went back to his apartment. Once again, as soon as he set foot inside, he felt someone must have been there. He checked the bedroom, the kitchen, and the bathroom, where he found a paper wrapping in the middle of the bathtub. He leaned over, tried to pick it up, but realized it was wet all over the bottom. It would have fallen apart if he'd picked it up. He opened the wrapping and couldn't work out at first what was inside: something was moving. He jumped back, afraid, not least because he'd seen a small red mark that looked like blood on the bottom of the bath, close to the wrapping, which had meanwhile started moving by itself. He decided to get a brush and dustpan, to slide the thing onto it and throw it out of the window without even looking to see what it was. He went to the kitchen and found what he wanted. As he was leaning over the wrapping once again, he couldn't stop himself peering inside for a second time and immediately realized that what was moving was a tiny jumble of newborn animals, maybe kittens heaped one on another, still wet and encrusted with blood, busily twisting their little blind faces, trying to struggle free from the tangle.

He moved away from the bathtub, began pacing about the house. As he passed the wardrobe he hurled his whole body against it and felt the noise of the timber that was starting to come apart. Then, without thinking, he began to sing to the music they were broadcasting on TV, but his voice died on his lips, like when you try yelling out when you're hurtling down on a swing that's being pushed as high as it will go. Pacing up and down, he tried to avoid pieces of the light bulb still on the floor, but could still hear the sound of fragments of glass being trampled under his shoes. This sound brought him back to reality. He took a plastic bag and inside it he put the wrapping he had found in the bathtub. He went out and threw it into the garbage chute on the landing.

When he got back, he turned off the TV and moved to the window. In the room of the house opposite, the blue balloon was still floating against the ceiling. The light had now been switched off and, in the blue light of the television, it seemed even larger. The woman was lying on her back on the couch and was absentmindedly running a hand through her hair. The child pulled down the balloon and, after disappearing for a while, went up to the woman. He took the balloon, holding it by the little knot at the bottom, and started hitting the woman on the face with it. He pointed the binoculars, saw the child and the woman were laughing. Then the woman took the balloon, holding it close to her body with both hands. The child started jumping onto the woman to get it back, lying on top of her as they fought, falling to one side or the other with the swollen curvature of the balloon compressed between the two bodies. The struggle lasted quite some time. Every so often the large immobile hand beside them, moving quick as lightning, slid in between the buttocks of the child busily fighting the woman, encouraging the two bodies to move ever more wildly and frantically.

The woman suddenly stopped, let the child take the balloon, and got up slowly from the couch. She went up to the window and stood still, peering toward him. A moment later she started to bang her forehead, bent double. From the movement of her mouth he realized she was shouting, though he heard no sound. He couldn't work out what was going on. He saw the woman rush toward the large hand. At once, pulling him by the arm, she dragged the man in front of the window. She was holding her hand up in his direction and her mouth kept moving frantically open and shut. He didn't know what to do. The room was dark, but the shutter was up. He slowly lowered himself, hoping that the movement would seem like a shadow playing on the window or like the sudden dropping of a garment placed on the handle of the window. As he was moving down, when only his eyes and forehead could be seen above the windowsill, he saw that the man was opening the window and the woman behind him continued waving her arm, pointing to something. Once below the windowsill, walking on all fours and with the binoculars in one hand, he moved to the farthest corner of the room, where he was sure it would be impossible to make out even his shadow. He pointed the binoculars and saw that the man was still leaning out of the open window, with his elbows on the ledge. The light was behind him, all that could be seen was the outline of his large, dark figure, which took up almost the whole blue rectangle of the window. Just behind him, still partially lit by the dim glow of the television, the woman was looking out as though panic-stricken.

He moved toward the bed, waited for a while, and, when he moved back to the window, saw the shutters of the apartment opposite were now all down, except for that of the storeroom, which seemed slightly up. He thought maybe this was a trap: they wanted to spy on him through the tiny holes between the slats that hadn't been completely lowered while he, imagining he was safe, revealed his presence openly in the darkness. There again, he couldn't even lower his shutter, nor lower it after having suddenly switched on the light in the room to make it seem he'd just returned home, which might have provoked unpredictable reactions in the house opposite.

He went back to the dark corner of the room and pointed the binoculars. It looked as though the shutter of the storeroom was now down, even though a gap between two slats not perfectly together would have been enough for them to see out. But maybe they were no longer thinking about him in the house opposite, maybe they were busy, now that no one could see them, taking hold of every object, passing it from hand to hand, from the balloon to the dishes, dishes and TV controls and genitals and toilet paper and water and the book laid on the nightstand and the light switch and lips and mucus and the air around two mechanisms in the darkness, one of which was rigid, resting on its elbows and on its toes, ready to plunge repeatedly into the other waiting with its legs open and slightly raised, like those chicken carcasses with their knees broken and bent a little behind, with a great gash, now completely hollow from its evisceration . . .

Whatever was going on, he didn't lower the shutter, and went to bed all the same. In the darkness, apart from the window, he saw one great flank of the building opposite and, higher up, the empty cabin of a tall crane. He closed his eyes almost at once but was woken soon after by the usual rustling that came from behind the wardrobe. An infinitely light sound crossed the entire room. He decided not to get up. Ten minutes later, he began to hear an endless, rhythmic groan from the room of the woman next door, and even in the middle of the night, when he got up to urinate, he could hear that sound returning in ever-fluctuating tones, uttered in small high-pitched howls after each new intrusion from the other low but relentless voice.

Next morning he got up early, bothered by the light that came in through the window. He was surprised when he saw the shutter was up. Then, looking down on the floor, he saw a piece of paper folded in four. It was close by and, to get it, all he had to do was sit up and reach out from the bed.

He picked it up, opened it and began to read:

So speaking he let fly. Athena guided the weapon
to the nose, near the eye; it pierced his white teeth,
the dauntless bronze severed his tongue at the base,
the point emerged from the tip of the chin.

Just below, after a small blank space, there was some more writing:

the jagged rock shattered both the tendons
and the bone; he fell backward into the dust,
stretching his hands out to his friends,
gasping for breath; but Peiros, the one who had struck
    him,
ran up and stabbed him by the navel with his spear;
his entrails poured over the ground; darkness immedi-
    ately covered his eyes.

He jumped out of bed, went toward the wardrobe. Passing in front of the window, he turned automatically to look at the building opposite and, in one of the windows, the storeroom window, in the gap left free by the shutter that was not completely down, he saw the motionless figure of the woman. Her chin and her forehead were hidden by the windowsill and by the lowest part of the shutter; only the central strip of her face could be seen. "She must be sitting on something very low," he thought, "or kneeling on the floor . . ."

He quickly dressed, moved to the farthest corner of the room, and, half hidden behind the back of a chair, pointed the binoculars: the woman's face was still there, staring in his direction. Her slightly swollen eyes and mouth suggested she had done a lot of crying. Her face suddenly vanished, the palm of a hand appeared for a moment, like an invitation to wait. Then the hand also disappeared and something moved, light in color. The back of the large packing box was brought toward the window. Then it stopped. The woman must have pushed it from behind, sliding it over the floor. After a rapid scissor movement, the patch of hair appeared between her splayed legs and soon after, in quick and no doubt calculated succession, a hand plunged several objects in among the hair: a shoelace first, then a light bulb, the end of which, the metal part, she introduced, slowly turning it with her hand, following the line of the thread. She left it like this for a few moments, like a suspended glass bubble. Having removed the shoe-lace and the light bulb, she introduced the prongs of a fork with great care. Slowly, she took these out as well. Then she dangled a deflated orange balloon against her vagina. She began pushing it in with one finger, pressing it inside. The other hand appeared with the toy pump. The two hands fumbled about for a while to fix the end of the balloon to the nozzle of the pump, then they gradually began pumping while the woman's body moved back, little by little, to lie on the box. From the rhythm of their movement that day, she seemed incapable of holding back. All of a sudden he saw her let go of the pump and thrust herself higher, while her hips moved as if under the impulse of an electric shock and her legs flailed and twisted about. The toy pump hung between her legs, slipped down from the box, dragging with it the tattered balloon, burst through who knows what movements of air inside the woman's body, now resembling an interminable colored thread that carried on flowing out. A moment later, the woman's face fell onto the box. He could see her mouth opening and closing, saliva trickling down in long dribbles. Then the woman stretched onto her side, crouched flat on all fours. With one hand she was gripping her throat, with the other she removed from her sex the last colored fragments of rubber that had torn inside her, while beneath her body, shaken by who knows what chain of explosions, her breasts swung slowly, as if nothing had happened.

Without realizing, he had crossed the whole room and was now in front of the window. And he was right in front of the window when the woman's body rolled down from the box. Before dropping onto the floor and vanishing from sight, a strip of white flesh had completely filled the narrow gap beneath the shutter, like the small part of a far larger body that entirely filled that room. Then the gap was suddenly empty: the weight of the body had most likely widened the space between the box and the portion of wall beneath the window and made room for itself as it fell into that narrow gap.

He dropped the shutter. The room fell into a semidarkness illuminated only by the irregular dots of light that came from the gaps between the slats that had not completely closed. He realized he was still holding, together with the binoculars, the note he had read a little earlier. He moved the wardrobe and slipped it under the door. He crouched on the ground to watch the sheet of paper from close up, ready to catch any slight movement that might indicate the presence of a hand on the other side. But the paper didn't move.

He stood up, went to the kitchen, then back to crouch in front of the door. He was holding a box of matches. He lit one, setting light to a corner of the paper that was sticking out from the crack. The paper began to curl as the flame spread, moving ever closer to the door. Now, faced with the danger that the flimsy wooden door might catch fire, whoever was on the other side would have to betray his presence, revealing himself with some sudden gesture, by pulling the paper out from under the door or blowing into the crack to put out the small fire. He bent down lower until his cheek was resting on the floor, moved a finger toward the crack under the door so that he would feel even the lightest waft of breath. But the flame stopped, seemed for a moment to go out, then passed to the other side of the narrow crack. From the tiny glow visible beneath the crack it seemed the paper was still burning to the end, without any breath coming from the other side to put it out, so far as he could tell.

He pushed the wardrobe back against the wall, took the milk carton from the refrigerator, and put it to his lips to drink. The milk tasted sour. He took the carton into the bathroom and began pouring it down the toilet. As it slowly arched down into the bowl, the water at the bottom, from yellowish as it was, turned increasingly white and impenetrable, as if the drain hole were no longer there and the glazed walls had completely sealed off the toilet without leaving the smallest way through. He spat several times to take away the taste of the sour milk, urinated, then flushed the toilet and, in the whirl it created, the milk and urine began to dilute before being swallowed into the pipe, leaving a small, transparent, shimmering puddle at the bottom.

Soon after, pacing up and down in the semidark room, he felt his strength returning. He raised the shutter a little to look through one of the tiny holes between the slats: there was no movement in the window of the apartment opposite.

He decided to go out. On the landing he met the neighbor, who was opening her door just then.

"Do you want to come in?" he heard her saying.

He shook his head.

"I'm alone, we can keep each other company for a while . . ."

"Maybe I'll come this afternoon," he answered.

But as he passed her to reach the stairs, she couldn't resist the sudden impulse to run a hand through his hair, sinking all of her fingers into it and tightening them for a moment around the top of his small skull. He felt a slight warmth of fingertips, while his scalp moved like a soft glove over of his skull bone. She had her back against the door of her apartment, had slipped her hand down for a moment beneath his jersey, feverishly clasping his shoulder and the base of his neck.

A second later she hurriedly withdrew her hand, went back inside.

He went down to the street and started walking. He turned into the tunnel, passing under the railroad tracks and away from the area. Close to the station, to his great surprise, he saw his car parked on one side of a small street. It had been there since he had left the single-room apartment after the death of the old lady. But he didn't think he had parked it in that exact position. Maybe it had been stolen and then abandoned, or those who clean the street had moved it with a tow truck.

He opened the door and climbed inside.

It was all just the same as before, no one had touched anything. Even the smell inside was unchanged. He tried to get it going, out of curiosity, though he was sure it wouldn't start. Yet the engine started straightaway. And so, as there was still some gasoline, he set off. He went through the streets of the center, left them behind, and began to drive through the wide suburbs. Every so often he stopped, sat there in the car looking out, then set off again. Toward midday he bought something in a store and ate sitting in the car, throwing the oily wrappings out of the window. After he had eaten, he set off again, and when he realized the gasoline was just about to finish he pushed down the clutch and let the vehicle glide a little farther on the asphalt, snatching another hundred yards. He pulled up by a sidewalk, got out, and headed home.

Once inside the apartment, he rushed to the window and pulled up the shutter: the apartment opposite seemed deserted. Passing in front of the wardrobe he thought about checking the door to see whether the burned paper was still under it or whether it had been blown away to clear the path in preparation for other shots. He moved the wardrobe: the burned fragments were still there. He didn't touch them. In that way he could check on the movements of the person on the other side of the door: if the fragments disappeared or moved position without any note being pushed through, he could be sure that someone had opened the door and entered the house from that side.

He pushed the wardrobe back against the door and went into the kitchen. There was something strange on one of the gas rings: it was a handwritten note, folded several times.

He picked it up. No one had been through the hidden door behind the wardrobe, so whoever had delivered it could only have entered the house by the front door.

He began to read.

3

So here we are, old friend . . . I already knew a few things about you.

From when we used to make those journeys together to certain, you might say, border areas . . . What long journeys! We couldn't even look each other in the eye!

But there was always something I couldn't figure out. Even later, after we'd lost touch. Over the past few days I've been able to keep a close watch on you, ever since I found you on the bench in that waiting room with the air of someone unable to account for anything or who lays traps while wandering in circles . . .

Why should I grovel in front of you?

Ever since you've been in my house I've had a constant opportunity to listen to you. The walls here are made of card, as you've discovered, and what's more, I have a small lookout point, I'm not telling you where. I've been told other things by your neighbor, with whom I spend some fairly lively nights, as you may have heard. Though I have a suspicion, for some reason that escapes me, that she doesn't tell me quite everything.

You'd prefer not to answer, of course. As for everything else, do you think I don't understand?

I know, I have to apologize for a few little surprises I've left for you these last few days. But the problem is something else. The problem is that you're a slaughterer, you're inside my house, and there's now nothing I can do about it.

So listen carefully to what I'm about to tell you: have you ever been lucky enough to spend any time watching a pig as it chews the rind of a watermelon? I have, yes, and for many years. Just by the house where I was born—the farmhouse, if you like—there was a pigpen half underground. You ought to hear what a sound! Musical, almost immaterial, even if it doesn't conceal the fact that the pig's teeth are relentlessly crushing and grinding the watermelon rind. It's a different, hypnotic sound. I always made sure I had the job of taking the watermelon rinds to the pigs, I'd stop there for a long while listening. That sound accompanied me all through my childhood, it always struck me as being full of a truth that no one can ever completely grasp. Behind that systematic and indifferent expression, the snout of a pig is a hell of a powerful grinding machine! Listen to this music for a while, my friend, I recommend it! You ought to grasp its novelty! It's an apple crushed by the heaviest and most lethal of presses. You ought to grasp its geometry! You're familiar only with the chewing of hungry cats that tear apart without a sound. The pig, on the other hand, allows a hint of music to saunter to its lips, come what may.

Have you understood now? So where do you think the paradox lies? Do you want us to talk about new times? We have put you out of a job and the audience can now only applaud.

So, what do you say? I reckon we'll be seeing each other again soon and maybe, it's up to you, we could spend a jolly evening together, sticking our tongues out so far that we can hold them under the sole of a shoe, then trample over them like inside a circle.

However it goes, where do you want to get to? Do you have something else in mind? I don't imagine so, therefore you have to stop provoking and continually throwing yourself into the fray. It could cost you dearly.

He dropped the piece of paper, rushed into the bedroom, and lowered the shutter. He started wandering about in the semidarkness, peering at the walls searching for the lookout point mentioned in the letter. But he could find nothing. "Maybe it was just a bluff," he thought, glancing all around the room. He also went to check the bathroom, especially the large electrical water heater over the bathtub. In one corner of the kitchen, between two brooms and a floor scrubber, he found a long bamboo pole on top of which a small brush had been tied for removing cobwebs from the ceiling. He cut the string with a knife, and the brush fell to the floor. He took the bamboo pole and carried it into the bedroom. He threw the mattress of the second bed onto the ground, dragging it in front of the wardrobe. He arranged it carefully on the floor, then lay on it, next to the bamboo pole. He began staring at the ceiling for an incalculable length of time, while the minuscule patches of light that reached him, filtering through from the shutter, gradually darkened and disappeared. "Now, in truth, no one can see me," he thought. And against his temple he felt a knot of the bamboo pole, like a head gently resting against his.

More time passed. He began to feel a coldness in his back that rose from the floor and passed through the thin upholstery of the mattress. He stood up. In the darkness he approached the door and went out.

Soon after, in the neighbor's house, sitting on a corner of the bed, he listened as she read from a book. She was wearing the usual bathrobe, which she held around her with both hands as though she were cold or sick. She sat at the other end of the bed, leaning slightly forward.

"Listen to this!" she said cheerfully.

The earliest remains of animal life in this area date back to the Upper Tertiary Period (Lower Pliocene, 12–8 million years ago). They are the remains of sea organisms embedded in bluish fine-grained mica clay.

Most of these are remains of shells (Gastropods and Lamellibranchiata) though there is no scarcity of other animal remains such as corals, bryozoa, fishes, cirripedia as well as vegetable remains like the impressions of leaves, wood, semicarbonized cones, pieces of bark . . .

Before leaving the neighbor's house again, among a pile of soiled laundry, he saw the nightgown used the previous day to collect the fragments of glass. While she was in the kitchen, he took it. He hurriedly rolled it up, and it was so light that he could slip it into a pocket.

Back in his house, everything seemed normal, nothing suggested that anyone had been in during his absence. Through the holes in the shutter he peered at the windows of the house opposite: they were now all closed, with no sign of light. "They might have gone out," he thought, "or could have already gone to bed."

He lowered the shutter, took the bamboo pole, and went to lie down. After a while he began to hear the usual moaning from the room next door, which had a tone that night of absolute desperation, like someone being forced to suffer a devastating surgical operation while still awake. But he now knew that, despite appearances, nothing final would happen even then, that this moaning would carry on for hours and hours, becoming more guttural and insistent in tone, like during a suffocation, and that it would all be repeated again the following evening and every evening after that, each time as if nothing had happened.

He lay awake. The dim light that filtered through between the slats of the shutter revealed the bright outline of the crib. Strange cries had been coming for some while from the neighbor's bedroom that sounded sometimes like sobs and sometimes like an interminable and provocative tortured laugh.

He got up and went to the window. He lifted the shutter and saw that outside it was already getting light. The shutters of the apartment opposite were still fully down. He went to lie on the bed. As he was searching for his handkerchief he felt a large bundle bulging in his pocket. He pulled it out: it was the neighbor's nightgown. He tried to straighten it, holding it at two different points and gently shaking it. Something small and rolled up, concealed in one of the folds of the nightgown, fell onto the floor. He bent down to look: it was a pair of men's underpants, entangled in the other larger garment. "This means the pile of laundry to be washed included the other man's clothes," he thought. "She must do them together with her own in a single wash . . ."

He gazed at the underpants without picking them up off the floor. The front opening was wide and one of the edges hung slackly, like a weak lower lip. There was a yellow tinge between the legs and blue in the pouch, with two perfectly light blue shadings on either side.

"He's someone who rarely washes," he told himself.

He lowered the shutter and went down to the street. No one was about, even the shops were still shut. He walked alongside the railroad tracks. He arrived at the station, went into the waiting room and stayed there a while, walked back and forth by the large illuminated newsstands, ate something at the hectic bar among several groups of departing travelers, then felt a sudden need to relieve himself. He went to the washroom and emptied his bowels in a few seconds. He left and started walking along the platforms. All of a sudden, from a tiny sound, he realized they must have switched on the loudspeakers in one of the many station offices. A moment later, in fact, someone cleared their throat, making a great noise. Then a voice began to emerge from all the loudspeakers, but unexpectedly, rather than announcing the arrival or departure of a train, it started saying:

When the sperm, driven by the movements of the flagellum, comes into contact with the egg cell, this emits a protuberance, called a "cone of attraction," through which the male element penetrates the egg plasma, generally leaving the tail outside, and it immediately heads toward the female pronucleus with which it fuses, thus generating a large diploid nucleus . . .

He moved back behind an overhang in the wall. He felt he was suffocating. "Not so loud!" he thought. "Everyone will hear!" Meanwhile, the voice carried on to explain:

At the same time, the surface of the egg thickens to stop the penetration of other sperm. Sometimes more than one sperm can penetrate, but it will always be just one male pronucleus that fuses with the female pronucleus.

From his lookout point he could see that the number of people waiting for the train had grown, had formed into small groups, busily talking. Someone, taking up what little space remained, had moved too close, as if through some unrestrainable sense of fellow feeling.

He felt overwhelmed by shame. Trying to avoid eye contact, he started to move back along the platform, left the station, and returned to the street. But even there he could still hear the metallic though somewhat muffled voice of the loudspeakers. And could still follow what it was saying.

He hurried away from the station area, almost running. His was panting for breath, he had to stop now and then, moving his arms in the air. Several blocks farther on, behind the glass of an automatic vending machine, he saw a pile of deflated balloons. As he searched his wallet, he realized his money was about to run out. He put a coin in the slot of the machine, turned a small metal handle, and a balloon dropped a moment later into the drawer at the bottom. He tried to blow it up a bit, to check it wasn't torn, then put it in his pocket.

Back home, he dropped onto the mattress on the floor

by the wardrobe and lay there for many hours wide awake. Then got up. Moving about in the semidark room, he went to get the bamboo pole, which was still propped against the wall by his bed. He looked for some string but could find none anywhere. There were just those few bits, now in pieces and of no use, which had kept the brush tied to the top of the pole. Trying to make as little noise as possible, he tore a bedsheet, made some strips out of it. He went into the kitchen to examine each of the knives in the drawer. Apart from those ordinary knives, there were some much larger ones with broad, almost square blades, like meat cleavers; others were long and rectangular. He chose one with a tough triangular blade. With the strips of sheet he began to bind its handle tightly to the top of the bamboo pole. He worked away for some time. To prevent the knife from moving, he bound both its handle and the tip of the pole with strips of sheet to strengthen the grip. Finally, to test its resistance, he thrust the knife into the floor, held on to the pole with all his weight, suspended in the air for several moments. Then he checked the knife again. It hadn't slipped an inch, even the point was intact. In the wooden floor, however, there was a small gash.

All at once he heard a small, almost imperceptible noise. More than a noise, it seemed like a flowing sound. He gazed around the dimly lit room but saw nothing. He looked at his feet: there was something liquid on the floor. He bent down without letting go of the pole, squatted on his heels, and realized something dark was floating on the liquid, maybe the bits of paper he had burned the day before under the door. Even the small fragments of glass, swept along by that small inundation, made tiny sounds as they moved. The liquid, whatever it was, was clearly coming out from beneath the door behind the wardrobe. It could just be water, he thought, but it could also be urine, or some kind of inflammable substance the other person would set light to from behind the door at the right moment, burning him alive inside the room. And, if it was just water, was it the contents of a glass, of a bottle, or the beginning of an endless flow that was streaming out from a rubber hose attached to an open faucet in the other room and aimed against the gap beneath his door? There must certainly be a lot of liquid, since it wasn't being absorbed by the mattress in front of the wardrobe and was flowing around it instead, advancing across the room. Not considering the fact that water conducts electricity . . .

Moving slowly so that his shoes would make the minimum of noise on the liquid film, he went to get the neighbor's nightgown and the male underpants. He left the room with these in one hand and the pole in the other. He hung the nightgown on the outer handle of the bathroom door and let the underpants fall on the floor, gaping and contorted. He went to the front door, turned the key, and opened it. He left it open for a moment, then shut it again loudly, with a bang. He turned the key once more in the lock, again from inside, and went quietly into the bathroom, leaving the door half open. He propped the pole against the wall, put one foot on the edge of the bathtub and the other on the washbasin, hoping this wouldn't collapse under his weight, and managed to grip the top of the large electric water heater. He pulled himself up with his arms and, by moving slowly onto it, he could gradually sit down, even though, restricted by the ceiling which forced him to remain squashed and to lean slightly to one side, he kept feeling he was about to fall forward. He thought, there and then, he would manage to stay like that for no more than a few minutes. He leaned back slightly and saw that the metal plate that held the water heater was fixed firmly to the wall. The hooks of three strong expansion bolts were in fact just visible. He let a few minutes pass: he felt sick, thought he was going to die at any moment without ever succeeding. He felt as though the large water heater was expanding, squashing him further against the ceiling. If he put his hand on top of it, he was in even more danger of falling forward. So it was better to jam his pelvis between the wall and the rear of the water-heater and then rest his feet in some way on two sides of the metal plate. Slowly he managed to take up his new position, gaining a little extra height in this way. Several long minutes passed. Moving his pelvis with caution, all the more since the water heater had begun to sway with each movement he made, he slipped a hand into his pocket and pulled out the balloon. He began to blow. As he slowly inflated the balloon, his body seemed gradually to get smaller, enough to hold out a little better in the small space between the ceiling and the top of the water heater. He knotted the balloon with the help of his teeth. He realized immediately, by chance, that by holding it with both hands he could place it over his head like a cushion, gaining more space and reducing the tension of the muscles and the tendons of the neck. He relaxed for a few moments, then stretched his hand toward the wall and slowly began to lift the bamboo pole. He held it firmly in his fist, leaning forward as he raised it toward the ceiling. It was almost entirely up when the knife tied to the end struck the electric light bulb that hung in the middle of the room. He froze. The light bulb swayed for a long while, giving a small hissing sound that seemed interminable. When it finally stopped, he waited still longer. He was afraid the blow might have damaged it. He knew it might shatter at any moment, when he least expected it, perhaps even just by looking at it . . . He finished lifting the pole. He was now almost perpendicular to the ceiling, leaning slightly. In order to support it he had fixed it between his elbow and the surface of the water heater, pulling it back as far as possible. The weight was rather more balanced that way. The strips of sheet that bound it hung down slightly frayed.

Some time passed, maybe a few minutes, maybe much more. He had left his watch out there and couldn't keep track. His body seemed to grow slowly accustomed to that position, or at least he was no longer aware of it. His head rested every now and then on the balloon, looking for the perfect balance in the middle so as not to be pushed by its curvature beyond the edge of the water heater. Those short intervals of rest were enough to send him off into dreams that lasted just an instant yet were exact in every detail. He was walking, for example, with a group of visitors along an unpaved avenue around a planetarium. Ahead of them was a guide. Next to him was someone he knew, and the perfectly trimmed hedges on either side seemed pure masses. Something very important happened, everyone was talking about it. Evening was approaching, and the air was warm but suffocating. The streets outside the gates were crowded with people. They were streets that went up- and downhill, teeming with so many people that they looked like moving pyramids. After a while they all went into the planetarium. The entrance hall was dark blue so as to accustom their eyes gradually to the total darkness. Only the silvery trails of the constellations could be seen. The inner surface of the screen inside was a great hemisphere that represented the celestial vault. The lights went out, and when the projection began a few moments later it already seemed like the open air of a clear night, and the celestial vault was the same that the first humans saw when they peered up at the heavens. Under the dome, in the center, two hemispheres at either end projected the fixed stars, while several disks pulled by motors, carrying projections of sun, moon and planets, made it possible to see the apparent orbits that these described across the celestial sphere, among the fixed stars . . .

He shook himself awake. The house was in complete silence. He dozed off again several times. Moving his arm slightly, he realized it was completely numb. He rested his cheek again on the balloon and noticed it was wet. Slowly, every now and then, he moved the hand that held the bamboo pole, careful not to let any of the knots rub against the balloon and make it burst. He couldn't be sure how long he had been up there. However long it was, he now knew perfectly well that he couldn't get down until the other had arrived.

Another eternity passed, which was perhaps only a few moments. All at once he heard a light metallic noise. It came from the bedroom. He froze, raised his head from the balloon. He heard another noise. It could only be the wardrobe being dragged across the floor, while the first may have been a key in the lock or a door handle turning. He waved the bamboo pole to check that he could still move his arm and hand. He thought for a moment that the other would see him hidden up there in the darkness and, having grabbed the pole, would pull him down, smashing his skull against the edge of the bathtub. There was a further silence, but he could feel the other was already inside the house. He pointed the top of the pole in the direction of the half-open door, and with the other hand he began to rub the surface of the balloon, which gave out a long, panting groan. In the bedroom, silence fell once more. In all likelihood the other person, attracted by the sound, had turned toward the toilet door, had already seen the nightgown hanging from handle and the underpants on the floor. His presence now felt infinitely close. Without the slightest noise, the outline of a head slipped through the half-open door. Maybe on seeing the last frayed strips of the bed-sheet hanging down in the dark, it turned slightly up to look in his direction. As his body, compressed between the ceiling and the water heater, thrust the pole down onto the temple of the intruder, he heard the voice of the other murmur with infinite surprise:

"What is it, up there?"

The pole encountered something hard as stone, after which he felt it plunge into an enormous mass that burst open, emitting a sound similar to that of a piece of wood being slowly and forcefully split. The other's head struck heavily against a wall, causing something to fall to the ground, while he too, losing his balance as he lunged with the pole, plummeted down, rolling over something hard, banging his knee and temple against the edge of the lavatory. The balloon, squashed or ripped by something in some part of the small room, burst, deflating with a hiss. For a moment he lost his senses. When he opened his eyes again, he realized his body, having been constricted for so long, was as good as dead in some parts. He had fallen to the floor, his legs not managing to support him.

He stretched an arm out to brace himself. All at once he turned.

The other's face was just a few inches away. His mouth, still drawn into a cold smile of astonishment, was moving imperceptibly, murmuring something incomprehensible. He began to roll across the floor to get away, jumping over something bulky and then moving farther away, covering his eyes instinctively with his hands, his head hunched between his shoulders.

Once inside the bedroom he gave out a high-pitched shriek, kept rolling and banging against furniture and chairs while, at that same moment, the doorbell started ringing wildly. He fell silent straightaway. As soon as he realized he could stretch out his limbs, he tried spreading himself out on the ground, trying not to crush the last remaining fragments of light bulb, and gradually, while someone continued ringing outside the door, he managed to lie down flat on the wet floor. The doorbell gradually stopped. He too began to breathe more slowly, suddenly aware of all the wetness in which he lay.

He remained there a long time. He felt the moisture on his back and head. When he lifted himself up a little to look about, he saw that the floor around him was almost completely dry, as if all the liquid had been absorbed by his body. He got up with great effort and went back to the bathroom. He switched on the light. The first thing he saw was the bamboo pole. Sticking out from the man's head, it crossed the small room diagonally. The man was sitting in a corner with his head against the wall. A light froth had appeared from his temple, all around the knife embedded in his skull. It was dripping onto the floor and into the tattered balloon that had flown there after it had burst.

The man's lips still seemed to be moving, continuing to mutter something though no sound emerged. And only when he had managed, after various failed attempts, to extract the tip of the pole embedded in the bones of the skull by pressing a foot against the man's neck and pulling with both arms, the mouth opened a little wider and a tiny sound came out resembling a sigh that put a final end to the insistent, indecipherable murmuring of before.

Two days later, as he was leaving the house in the first light of dawn, on noticing from a distance a trace of blood on the snow, he remembered all at once what had happened . . .

Having tipped the man's body into the bathtub, he had raised the bedroom shutter just a little. Through one of the usual windows opposite he could see the inert face of the woman staring in his direction. All the shutters were now fully up. The woman pressed her face against the glass, providing him with a strange distended image, with the nose squashed to one side and a vortex of flesh around two compressed lips, one of which was turned up on itself against the glass, which her breath was already beginning to mist up. Her face seemed to press ever harder against the glass, and he feared she would crash through it, cutting herself.

He hurried to the bathroom, used the tattered balloon

to mop up the clear stuff that had trickled onto the floor. Looking at it more closely he could see it was brain matter. He threw it into the toilet, flushing it for a long while because a fragment was stuck to the glaze some distance from the jet of water. As it still didn't want to go down, he poked it with a finger to detach it. At this point the doorbell rang again. He stopped flushing and stayed still. "It will be the neighbor," he said without saying a word. The body in the bath hadn't lost a drop of blood. Only the brain continued trickling from the side of the temple. Having put the plug in the hole, he opened the faucet. As the water gradually rose, the man's body shifted and moved in silence, as if almost alive. He closed the faucet and covered the body with several sheets of newspaper found on a shelf. He scattered them over its entire length, and over it he put other things he'd found in the kitchen: several potatoes, an onion, coffee powder and some sour milk. Then he ran to the window to look through one of the holes in the shutter with his binoculars. The woman's face was still there, squashed behind the opaque halo of glass.

He didn't go back to the bathroom for the rest of the day. Toward evening he urinated in the kitchen, then switched on the TV. But the picture was disturbed, hardly visible: appearing behind a mesh of constantly intersecting lines was the intermittent form of a hand busily pouring water over a still and almost shiny face. They were probably a few shots from a publicity break. Straight after, the picture was obliterated by a sudden rushing of waves that covered the slightest hint of sound. He turned off the TV and moved toward the shutter. Through the window opposite, the woman was now slowly moving about in the room. She seemed very tired, was walking with her head bent, pressing a hand against her stomach. He went to bed and, as soon as he dropped to sleep, snow began falling outside and there was not a sound from the neighbor's room and even the bathroom was completely silent while the man's brain carried on slowly trickling from his temple, gliding over a potato that floated in the water. And maybe too, in the rooms next to his, there was no one clinging to the wall at that moment like a transparent membrane.

Next morning, once awake, he went to the window and saw that everything outside was white with snow. Though it was very early and no one was yet about, the woman was already there at the window, squatting down in a corner. The bottom part of her face was hidden by the coating of snow on the window ledge. He rested the binoculars against the shutter, inadvertently knocking one of the slats. And perhaps the imperceptible movement had been enough to signal his presence to the woman, who suddenly opened the window.

He moved away from his lookout point. In the bathroom he checked the body sprawled out in the bath: the newspapers, growing wetter and wetter through the night, had stuck to the man's clothes and face at several points. On a potato under an armpit not completely immersed in the water, a tiny bud had sprouted. Everything else was just as before. Only the brain, which seemed to be seeping endlessly, had continued to trickle over the newspapers and into the man's gaping mouth.

He took the potato stuck beneath the armpit and went back to the bedroom: the woman was still at the open window and was perhaps protecting herself from the cold by kneeling on the floor and pressing her body against the radiator beneath the windowsill. Having lifted the shutter halfway, in full sight of the woman, he hurled the potato in through the window opposite. He lowered the shutter again and, looking through the holes with his binoculars, he saw her pick the potato up from the floor, examine it, and, having found the bud still undamaged despite the impact, hold it against her cheek.

The doorbell rang again, just once. Standing behind the door, he could hear footsteps move away. Then, rummaging on the bathroom shelf, he found several bottles of bleach and acid for cleaning the toilet. There was also, who knows why, some weed killer. He poured it all into the bathtub a moment before rushing out of the bathroom. He went back behind the window: the woman, standing still, seemed not to want to leave her place. He then ran back to the bathroom and, covering his nose with a handkerchief, sank his fingers under one of the man's eyes. But pushing it here and there, he couldn't manage to rip it from its orbit. He went to get

217

a kitchen fork and managed with this to tear out the long peduncle and the small connective muscles. He removed a few fragments of newspaper which, on drying, had become stuck to the eyeball. He took the slingshot and put the eye into its leather pouch. Then, having lifted the shutter again, he took aim and shot it through the window opposite.

The woman looked confused for a moment. The eyeball, having hurtled across the room, had hit a wall before rolling under the couch. The woman turned, used her handkerchief to wipe a small trace of blood from the wall, then squatted in front of the couch and, bending down, looked at the object underneath it.

In the early afternoon she went out onto the small balcony at one corner of the building. She remained there, looking out for a very long time despite the cold, and as she stood clinging to the rail, staring toward his shutter, he could see with his binoculars that some blood was trickling down her legs. He could distinguish the droplets that fell one by one onto the edge of the balcony, which, seen from an angle, seemed as thin as a sheet of paper, totally inadequate to support the weight of the woman who maybe hadn't made it collapse only because her body was gradually dropping in weight through the loss of blood, no doubt a result of the explosion inside her three days before.

Toward evening he noticed that small decorations had been hung from several windows of the building opposite in preparation for the approaching festivities. More had been put up by suppertime. A few dangling heads could be seen, busy moving small hands and colored paper chains.

He went to sleep, but after a few hours he woke, staring for a long while into the darkness. He pulled up the shutter. Much more snow had fallen, and he reckoned he could jump from the window without hurting himself. New decorations with metallic reflections hung here and there from the building opposite, and certainly no one else was keeping watch behind any of those open shutters. He went into the bathroom: the body, corroded by the acid, had changed color here and there. In particular, the flesh of the hands, immersed in the liquid, appeared stained in several places. The clothes, however, seemed much lighter, began to disintegrate.

Returning to the bedroom, he suddenly glimpsed the outline of the woman, standing in the darkness through the open window. He rushed back to the bathroom and tried two or three times to lift the body, taking hold of it by its clothes, which tore, however, more and more. In the kitchen he took a knife and some pruners, and as he was using them to open the body in the bath, turning out the bundle of intestines, an infernal smell was released from the great gash. He rushed out, bathed a handkerchief in vinegar and tied it behind his neck so that it covered his nose and mouth. In a corner beneath the sink he found some plastic bags. The walls of the house, he reckoned, would not have withstood the impact of that immense stink. He went back inside, ripped out something round, slippery, and fat, and tipped it into one of the bags. He had to pull and then cut several veins with the knife, sliding his hands into the tangled mass. He ran once more into the other room and, having whirled the bag round and round, he flung it toward the window opposite. But a moment later it fell to the ground, into the snow. "It was too light," he thought, "hungry dogs and cats will see to it that what's inside will disappear . . ." He went back into the bathroom, opened the body further, while the pruners were continually getting jammed in the jumble of dead flesh, slimy liquid, and shreds of clothing now burned by the acid. He took hold of something large and by pulling, and with the help of the knife, he managed to rip out a piece of lung. He put it into another bag along with the transistor radio, to increase the weight. In the other room he whirled the package round and round before launching it, and this time it went straight through the open window opposite. The bag was swallowed up by the darkness behind the woman, who turned back into the room. He pointed the binoculars: the woman had now put the transistor radio and the piece of lung on the window ledge. She switched on the radio and even from his window he could distinctly catch the sound of a song being sung in a foreign language, broadcast from who knows what part of the world, where someone, perhaps alone in a radio station and still half asleep, by lifting a small lever had just switched on all the systems producing a soft, gentle mechanical vibration, like a great live purring animal . . .

The woman rested her cheek on the piece of lung and stood still for some time as the radio played. Then he realized she had finally fallen asleep.

He stood watching her for a while, then went into the bathroom. The open body seemed to have expanded even further in the bathtub, changing shape and color, and a thousand liquids and streaks had unfurled from within it.

He left the house at the first light of dawn. Before going downstairs, he quietly hung the nightgown on the handle of the neighbor's door. At that same moment he heard the noise of something tearing itself apart. It came from the bathroom of the house he had just left. He stood there for a moment, immobile, appalled: maybe the body in the bath had exploded, hurling its internal liquids far and wide, propelling the intestine outside the window, maybe the stench had demolished every wall and door, or maybe it was the toilet light bulb that had simply burst in the now empty house.

He hurried downstairs, to the street. And it was then that he noticed the trace of blood in the snow at the foot of the building opposite, exactly below the woman's corner balcony...

He turned at once toward the frontage of the building he had just left: he was afraid he would see festoons of Christmas entrails hanging from his window...

But it was all quite normal.

He turned back and started to walk, hurrying away from that place.

There were more and more festoons beneath the windows, and the snow compacted beneath his feet, accompanying his steps with a syncopated swish. He took one of the wide streets that led to the center. There the decorations were even larger, sparkling, crossing the whole street, dropping almost low enough to touch the first automobiles that were starting to flow.

Where now could he disappear, he thought. Was there any such place in the world? Where silence began? Was it still so far away?

At a large junction he took another road, heading toward the station.

The King

I was so small then that I had to stand on my tiptoes to see things.

I wandered about inside a grand house full of skylights, fireplaces, steps, stairways, coats of arms. I looked out of a window, looked down at the bustling courtyard full of nobles who came out from their front doors.

Two other houses overlooked the same courtyard, where many nobles went about on foot or motor scooter and sometimes even on horseback, stiffly, on certain special occasions, when nobles who lived in other cities came to visit them. They came out all together into the courtyard dressed in ceremonial clothes brought out from the black chests on the stairways, and I also used to see a little boy my own age, with whom I had just been playing in the mud, as he too walked about in his little tailcoat, stiffly, pale-faced. The horse too was brought out from the stable inside the henhouse. A nobleman in ceremonial dress would climb onto it. From up there, he carried on talking to others below, who walked alongside, while the horse lifted its tail and let its pats drop to the ground. Once I even saw the little boy of my age on it, put there by his father so that he would learn to sit on a saddle while he was still young. The boy refused to open his eyes because he was frightened up there, while the horse moved at walking pace around the yard. He cried and shouted: "Papa, papa, let me down!" And his mother, Donna Paresi, went to the window of her room and told her husband to put the child down. But Conte Sauro said no, he had to learn, children had to be put up there while they were still young, like his father had done to him, that nobles have to ride horses.

In one of the houses overlooking the courtyard there lived an old count ill with asthma, Conte Vasco. He was always in bed and composed poetry in rhyme and meter that he sometimes read to me, lifting his head from the pillow between one attack and another, when I went to visit him in his house.

"Sit yourself here!" he said in his strained voice. "Next to my bed, and I'll read you a poem."

And he also added a name when he addressed me, my name, I suppose, most certainly! Though I don't remember what name I had.

He told me the history of the nobility and the origins of those who lived in the three houses that overlooked the courtyard.

"You see," he said breathlessly, "all the people who live in these houses . . . who walk around the courtyard in their stiff old-fashioned clothing, and then, the day after, in their normal torn jackets and unbuttoned trousers or on the horse with its mane covered with feathers because the hens have perched on its head in the henhouse . . . who ride for hours and hours around the long garden in Galletto's saddle . . . Tilde, Marchesa Nivea, before she falls into her deep sleep, Marchesa Daria, my wife, who is now deaf as a doorpost, my two daughters, Contessa Mia and Contessa Sua, who still use the bedpan as a bidet and work in the office of that lawyer of lost cases who sometimes walks about with his pocket linings out, who forgets to button his trousers when he leaves the brothel at night . . . Conte Stinco, who rides our steed Galletto, and then all the nobles who live in your house, in the other, Donna Paresi, who paints little flowers in watercolors, Conte Sauro, your little friend, his sister, Contessina Cecia, who is still so sweet, so childlike . . . the two twins who every so often cut off a piece of their body when they get it into their heads that they're not exactly alike in some detail, the old man himself, whom you see here, always in bed in the semidarkness, who writes his stupid compositions in rhyme and meter . . . Well, we are the heirs of the noble warriors who came down with the earliest hordes of Germanic tribes from Pannonia, with Alboin, heirs of the military dukes, of the great landowners with their villas, and of those at the head of the Carolingian counties, of the marquises that ruled their marches, of margraves, of barons who shut themselves up in their castles, of counts, of dukes, military leaders, and army generals who administered justice on behalf of the Emperor, the only ones free and entitled to carry military command. Those you see in this courtyard included descendants of Carolingian nobles, of fighting orders, German knights, Templars, descendants of Lombard warriors, of Barbarossa's noblemen, of Genoese warrior consuls, of the new Venetian nobility, members of the Morosini, Dandolo, and Mocenigo families, of the counts of Tuscia, of Contessa Matilde. And there are those who come from a branch of Ghibelline nobility, Conte Stinco, for example, whereas Donna Paresi is a Guelph. Doges' wives who vie with Greek queens and Persian empresses. You can see all this in their expressions, in the bone structure of their faces. Don't you see that certain faces are Germanic, others Viking, Scandinavian, while others clearly come from Asia Minor, from the Eastern Roman Empire? They all walk in the courtyard, around the garden, these families that come out of the mists of time . . ."

He began to cough, searched for a handkerchief on the pillow, started spitting catarrh into it, violently, always seemed about to suffocate. He coughed so loudly that even Marchesa Daria could hear. She rushed into the room, lifted his head to let him breathe.

"You go now!" she said. "The Conte needs to rest!"

I went for a while to the other boy's house. I had a look

inside the kitchen to see if anyone was there, stuck my nose inside the hoist that took the food from the kitchen to the first floor, where the dining hall was. I climbed up the stairway, wandered around for a while in the rooms, the yellow room, the green room, took the corridor as far as the bed chambers overlooking the courtyard, where the twins and my friend sleep. There were always small traces of blood here and there.

"What have you cut this time?" I asked the twins.

They happily showed me the point where they had cut themselves. Sometimes it was just a pimple that had appeared on one but not the other, other times it was something larger and more humid. They had once were once rushed to hospital when one of the twins sliced off a piece of his calf because it seemed larger than that of the other, and the other cut away a piece of his tongue because it looked longer. Every so often, loud cries could be heard coming from their room, and someone would ask: "What's happened now?"

And someone else would reply: "The twins! They've cut themselves again!"

I went back across the courtyard, back to my house where there were also many nobles, so many that I didn't even know them all. Including Marchesa Nivea, who was pregnant and always slept with a bag of ice on her belly. There were many others who didn't even see me, and whom I don't remember either. And also a little girl called

Piumetta, daughter of the woman who did the ironing, who had one leg thinner and shorter than the other because of polio, and wore an iron brace to support her. She rushed around the house, so fast that the sound of the iron could even be heard from far away. She was always lively, danced in front of me when I put a large slate disk on the gramophone turntable. The arm with the needle went into the groove, notes started coming out as if by magic, sounding through the whole house. The little girl ran to listen, began dancing alone in the middle of the room, for me, just for me, hopping about with her brace on the wooden floor. Sometimes she even peed on the ashes that were still warm in the fireplace with the coat of arms in the dining hall, to get my admiration.

She would call me, from there inside. At first I didn't see her.

"Piumetta, where are you? I can't see you!"

"I'm here, in the fireplace!"

I'd look about in the half-light until I saw her.

"What are you doing?" I asked.

"Peeing!"

"But people pee in the toilet!"

"And I pee in the fireplace!"

In the darkness beneath the chimney, that bright trickle could be seen coming from her body and ended in the warm ash.

"Now kiss me here!" she said, excited, after.

I had to go into the fireplace and kiss that naked smelly little thing, wet with pee.

And there was another little voice that called me. It came from inside the belly of the Marchesa Nivea, who always slept in the blue room. It was a thin, slight little voice, far away, that seemed to come from who knows where.

"Come here! Come here!" the little voice would say, as I was wandering the rooms of that big house.

"But where are you?" I asked looking about.

"I'm here."

"Here where? I don't see you."

"I'm in the belly of the Marchesa."

I went to the blue room, peeked inside. The Marchesa was lying in her bed, or on the striped couch beneath Conte Alano's ceremonial sword fixed to the wall, and was sleeping, sleeping, white as a sheet, exhausted, with the bag of ice on the dome of her belly.

I approached, not making a sound. I put my head against the dome, close to the Marchesa's hand that was holding the bag of ice, even as she slept.

"Here I am!" I murmured.

"I call, I call, but no one hears me!" the little voice said after a while.

"That's not true. I hear you," I said. "What do you want?"

"It's cold in here!"

"Of course it's cold! The Marchesa has to keep the bag of ice on her belly!"

"But why?"

"Because she has typhus. That's what the doctor said."

It said no more. I didn't know whether to go or remain.

"Are you still there?" the little voice asked, after a while.

"Yes, of course!"

"I feel cold," the little voice repeated. "It's all cold in here, freezing. How am I going to develop?"

Sometimes a hawk flew over the courtyard.

Conte Vasco knew everything, even though he never got out of bed. He knew all that was going on in the courtyard and in the three houses. Every so often he tried to get up, but it was enough for him to sit on the edge of the bed and stand on his feet for a moment and take a few steps on the creaky old wooden floor, with his long, skinny, white, bare feet, and he immediately had an asthma attack and had to go back and lie down.

"What are you doing? Are you crazy?" Marchesa Daria said as she hurried in.

"I want to go to the door! To see the courtyard, after so long!" said the Conte, fighting for breath, his eyes wide with the effort. "Give me the moleskin cloak!"

"You're out of your mind sometimes!" the Marchesa replied in despair, putting him back in bed.

Conte Vasco laughed, wheezing, like a naughty boy. The only sound in the room for some while was his breathing, like bellows.

The cloak was a large coat with an old worn moleskin lining. But everything else had a name different from those generally used, in that courtyard, or a name that hadn't been in use for some time. The enema, for example, was the "clyster," a hat was "the crown," a steak was "the assumption," shit "the ordure."

Conte Vasco's breathing gradually settled down, leaving just a hollow rattle that accompanied his words, when he was able to talk once more.

"We have spent it all!" he said. "Conte Astolfo, our father, enjoyed the high life. All that's left is this courtyard, the three houses, plus a few villas here and there, farmhouses, stables, dairies, rice fields. Conte Astolfo used to go to Paris two or three times a year. Women, horses . . . He gambled his estates at the casino. He had a passion for horses. Once he bought a horse that cost him a fortune. It arrived here in the courtyard after a long journey. I was still a child but I remember perfectly what happened. All the nobles outside their houses. All around the horse, to touch it, to admire it. Some felt it here, some patted it there. The horse's whole body trembled just on being stroked. When the groom tried to put on the bridle, they realized it had a serious defect to its tongue: it was twisted on itself like a corkscrew, the bit wouldn't go in its mouth. I can't tell you what happened in the courtyard that day! But the Conte wouldn't hear reason. He went back to Paris, squandered what was left of his wealth on women. He was a permanent guest in the high-class brothels and bars, knew even the Comte de Toulouse-Lautrec, La Goulue, Valentin le Désossé, Yvette Guilbert. He was there when Comte de Toulouse-Lautrec challenged to a duel someone who had dared to insult one of his painter friends whose name I don't recall, who drank absinthe and starved to death . . . He grabbed a sword that was larger than him, wielded it over his dwarf body, staring his adversary in the eye through his pince-nez spectacles. They too would stroll in the courtyard, around the garden, when they came here to visit Conte Astolfo. They stayed for months. Lunches, dinners, ribaldry . . . Comte de Toulouse-Lautrec on his little dwarf legs. And before that, there was Conte Manzoni, Conte Leopardi, Conte Alfieri, earlier still Matteo Maria Boiardo, Durante degli Alighieri long before, who was part of the ancient Florentine nobility, Sordello da Goito with his mistress, the sister of Ezzelino da Romano . . ."

"And you saw them all?"

"Of course I saw them!"

"But how old are you?"

He began to cough convulsively from the buildup of catarrh. He tried to pick up the thread of the story but was struggling for breath, choking.

"Who is the head of all the nobles?" I asked.

"The King!" he replied, when he was able to breathe again.

"And where is the King?" I asked.

"He's in exile."

"In exile? But where?"

"In a country far away. He sits overlooking the ocean."

"And why is he in exile?"

"Because they banished him!"

"They banished him? And who can banish the King?"

Conte Vasco shook his head.

"He cannot return to his own country, rule over us all, reestablish the royal court . . ."

"But why not?"

He started coughing violently once more in an effort to breathe, it was suffocating him.

Marchesa Daria hurried in, sent me away.

I went out into the courtyard. Passing in front of the henhouse, I heard the horse banging its hooves on the ground to send off the chickens.

One day, as I was hanging from the iron bar in the corridor, up from the floor, the doorbell suddenly began to the ring.

"What are you doing up there?" the ironing woman asked.

"I'm swinging."

She walked by, as I continued hanging from the bar, and went to open the door.

After a while I heard the footsteps of Piumetta, who was hopping along to see, as she was always curious.

Then the house went quiet.

"Who was it?" I asked from the bar, when Piumetta went past again.

She started to laugh.

"Why are you laughing?" I asked from up there, without losing hold of the bar.

"Because he stammered."

"Who?"

"The boy who came to ring the bell."

"And what did he stammer?"

"I...I...I...I'm...I'm here...t...t...to..." Piumetta started laughing even louder.

Then she ran off.

I remained there swinging. Through the nearby window, at an angle, I could see the end of the courtyard and the garden. The ironing woman had gone down and was walking all excited toward Conte Vasco's house. She was there for a while, then came out. She went to Conte Sauro's too. She stayed there for a while, then came back home. She passed me again, I could see she was going to try to wake Marchesa Nivea in the blue room.

I waited for her to leave, and for the Marchesa to go back to sleep. Then I went to her room. I approached the dome of her belly.

"Psst...psst..." I whispered.

"Who is it?" asked the little voice from inside.

"It's me. Who else could it be!"

"What do you want?"

"Someone came and rang at the door."

"Yes, I heard the doorbell too, a long long way from inside here."

It said no more.

"What are you doing? Are you still there?" I asked again, after a while.

"It's all cold, freezing in here," it kept complaining. "I don't know how to get warm."

Then I heard someone approaching and quickly moved away from the belly, with not even enough time to say goodbye to the little voice inside.

It was Conte Alano who entered. I went back to hanging from the bar in the corridor.

The boy came back a few days later. This time he also went up to talk to Conte Alano in his study, but from down below it was impossible to work out what he was saying with all that stammering.

"I'll . . . c . . . c . . . come . . . b . . . back tomorrow . . ." was all I could understand before he said goodbye to the Conte.

He left the house and then I could see him for the first time as he slipped back down the rear steps outside. He was thin, lopsided, had a wisp of hair that covered his eyes, a pancake nose, was slightly hunched with fear, like a young timid animal, didn't know where to put his hands.

As the ironing woman held the door open, he saw me there and turned to look at me.

Then he hurried down the steps. I went back to the corridor. From one of the windows I could see the boy going this time to ring at Conte Vasco's door and then also to Conte Sauro, and came out later, from there too, scratching his wisp of hair, red-faced.

He returned the following day. He stayed longer in each of the three houses.

"What does that boy still want?" I tried asking Piumetta, because she went up to eavesdrop and always knew everything.

"Wh . . . wh . . . wh-who . . . who knows!" she replied laughing, as she pulled up her dress to pee in the fireplace.

I left the house, crossed the courtyard, went to see Conte Vasco, but he was asleep. Then to my friend's house, but my friend wasn't there, and Conte Stinco was in his office, and Donna Paresi was painting a posy of flowers and didn't reply, Conte Sauro was shaving and couldn't speak so as not to cut himself, the two twins were fixed to the mirror, each peering at a nostril to check whether they were exactly alike or whether one of them had to be widened with a pair of scissors, it was impossible to find out anything from Contessina Cecia because she started giggling after two words and no longer made any sense.

I went back home. I couldn't even go and speak to the little voice because Conte Alano was in the room, busy talking to Marchesa Nivea in her state of deep drowsiness, whom only he could manage to wake every now and then.

I went to look out from a window and could see the hawk flying in the air above the courtyard.

"Hawk, hawk!" I called out. "Come down! Come to me! I'm here!"

No one said a word, but I could see the whole house was in a state of excitement. Everywhere there was someone sweeping, dusting, polishing, cleaning. The old carpet on the main stairway was changed, a new, red, freshly cleaned carpet was put down, which had to be stretched hard by two people so that it covered the whole length and could be fixed at the base of each step with its newly polished rod, because it had temporarily shrunk from being washed. Even the window panes had been washed and then wiped dry, the curtains had been changed. A man climbed onto a ladder to get up to wash inside the skylight, while another was doing the same thing on the roof. And there were chests wide open everywhere, from which bedcovers, curtains, rugs were being pulled out. As well as cupboards of clothing, and of crockery, from which plates and crystal glasses were being removed, and silver cutlery, each piece in a small, white cloth wrapping, indicating that an important dinner was to be held in the hall with the coat of arms over the fireplace.

"So what's going on?" I kept asking.

But everyone was too busy to stop to answer.

Meanwhile, the same preparations were going on in the other two houses, because I could see people through the windows going back and forth carrying great bundles of bedsheets and covers, moving furniture, polishing mirrors.

"What's going on?" I tried asking in the other houses too, but they didn't even seem to see me. I even once stopped the twins' wet nurse, who still went to the house even though the babies she had once suckled had now grown up. The wet nurse was hurrying along the corridor because she had been urgently summoned by the twins, who were very fond of her and often sought her advice, and now for example they needed to know from her whether their ears were identical in shape and whether the difference to be seen was simply caused by a defect in the mirror. But she managed to give me a quick answer all the same, as she hurried along because the twins were desperately yelling out for her from their room.

"An important person's due to arrive!" she said.

"But who? Who?" I tried asking her again, but she was already a long way away, in the twins' room, and I could hear she was doing all she could to calm them, reassuring them that the two ears were perfectly identical in shape, pleading with them to put down the scissors that one of the twins was holding to cut around the edge of his ear.

"Nurse, we trust you!" he heard them shouting in their room. "But are you really sure? You're not lying to us?" ·

And nor did my friend answer, not even when he and I were alone and we were seesawing on the usual plank balanced on a trestle left by the builders in one corner of the courtyard. We sat astride the plank, one at one end and one at the other. We started swinging in the air. One went up, the other down, then the first went down and the other up. We had to grip the plank tightly between our legs so as not to fall, and in the end there were always little white splinters, from the cement dust, to be pulled from the skin.

And not even then did my friend answer, not even when I asked him while he was up, at that moment when you're gripped by that uncontrollable fit of excitement.

"Who is it who's due to arrive?" I asked him from below.

He looked at me, his eyes intoxicated by the height and the thrill, but he didn't answer.

"Who is it who's due to arrive?" I tried asking him instead when he was down and I was up.

Still no answer.

He straightened his folded legs once again, gave a little push, the position once more reversed.

"We're friends!" I said. "You can tell me!"

"It's a secret," he replied at last. "No one must know. I have sworn."

"Well, who is due to arrive?" I went to ask Conte Vasco too.

"It's a secret! It's a secret," he whispered, out of earshot of the Marchesa, who had just left the room to empty the bedpan into the commode in the bathroom.

Then the Marchesa returned, and I left.

"Do you know anything?" I asked Piumetta.

"I know everything! I know everything!" she answered as she rushed off, hopping along on her brace.

But I couldn't decide whether it was true or whether she was just saying it because she was vain.

Even the little voice kept quiet when I approached the dome of the belly to talk to it.

"Someone's due to arrive," I whispered to it.

But the little voice inside made no answer.

"Have you gone deaf?" I asked, since maybe its little ears had frozen and it couldn't hear any longer.

There was no answer, the only sound to be heard was of Marchesa Nivea breathing, fast asleep.

"Who is due to arrive?" I asked again.

Silence.

Only after a while, when I was already a few steps away, did I seem to hear a soft, soft little sound coming from inside, and it was hard to work out whether it was the little voice crying in the frozen belly or the last remnants of heat unleashed from its little body crackling in the cape of its amniotic liquid as it froze.

Wandering about in the courtyard, I was trying to catch some of the words being exchanged between the people strolling around the garden, but they were talking so fast that it was impossible to figure what they were saying and, what was more, they were drowned out by the deafening noise of Galletto, the horse belonging to Conte Stinco, who kept turning about at a speed more rapid than usual, his face numb with emotion.

"Who is due to arrive?" I tried asking Conte Vasco again, while the room was empty and the only sound to be heard was his breathing in the semidarkness.

He made no reply. His chest could be seen going up and down beneath the blankets in his struggle to take in enough air at each breath.

"It's a secret!" he replied at last.

"But I know how to keep secrets!" I told him.

"Do you promise?"

I nodded yes, kissing two fingers that I placed across my mouth.

The Conte strained his head up from the pillow to make sure my oath had been carried out correctly. He looked around him two or three times, listening out to check that Marchesa Daria was in a room far away and couldn't hear.

He motioned for me to come even closer.

I moved my ear to the opening of his mouth struggling to breathe.

"The King is coming!" he announced.

I jumped back, not least because a second later Conte Vasco had started gasping more heavily, uncontrollably.

"The King? Here? Coming here?" I tried asking when the Conte's breathing had settled somewhat.

"Yes, here," he replied in a murmur, signaling for me to keep quiet, with a finger to his lips.

"But wasn't he banished?" I asked again.

"Yes, but he's returned secretly, traveling incognito, is

already back in his country, so we must say nothing. He has sent his servant on ahead to prepare us gently for the great news . . ."

"That boy who stammered?"

"Yes, he came to prepare the ground, to announce the King's arrival."

"But when will he be here?"

The Conte turned toward me, his neck strained, his eyes almost out of their sockets with the effort to breathe and the emotion.

"Tomorrow," he replied at last.

"Tomorrow?"

"Yes, he's already close! He crossed the border secretly, through woods, by night. And he'll be with us tomorrow. We're preparing to welcome him, we'll all come to the hall of arms to have dinner with him, we'll all come out of our houses to pay homage to our King. I too will get out of my bed, I'll dress in my tailcoat, throw my moleskin cloak over it, leave my house, cross the courtyard, climb the stairway, reach the great hall ready-laid with glasses glinting on the tablecloths, the cutlery, the fire burning in the fireplace, the sound of sparks rising up into the blackened chimney, all of us standing, nervously waiting for the arrival of our King, in our places, in our finest clothes. With a grand gesture I'll pull off my moleskin cloak, I too will take my place with the rest of my family, before our King, at last, face-to-face, I too will stretch out my hand, our fingers will touch, we will shake hands, our women will curtsy to him, blushing with emotion, and I too will bow, and Conte Alano, Conte Sauro, Donna Paresi, all the others, the twins too, neatly trimmed for the occasion, they too in tails, and Marchesa Nivea too, if she manages to wake from her sleep . . ."

Conte Vasco suddenly paused. He started breathing heavily, very heavily, his mouth wide open after his long discourse. But fortunately the Marchesa was in a room far away and couldn't hear.

"But why here?" I asked again, when his breathing had calmed a little.

Conte Vasco turned his eyes toward me. They glistened.

"Yes, here, he's coming here, to us!" he replied. "Of a thousand noble families and a thousand courts he has set his eyes on us, has chosen us, our houses, our courtyard, to return secretly to his country from where he was banished, and to speak through us to all the nobility of the country, of the world . . ."

The dining room glittered, cutlery and glasses sparkled on the layers of tablecloths, the fire burned in the fireplace. I wasn't among those invited because I was too little and my hands wouldn't reach up to take things from the table. Piumetta, the ironing woman's daughter, wasn't there either, because she couldn't be. But the sound of her leg brace was heard everywhere. She went to peep here and there, then hopped off. I was in the main kitchen and tried to see something from the service hatch, slipping my head into the space that cleared from time to time between the crush of hands and arms and piles of serving dishes and soup tureens that kept being passed inside. Through those gaps I could see the outlines of the guests standing still in the hall, waiting. All the nobles of the three houses around the courtyard were dressed differently, unrecognizably: Donna Paresi, Conte Alano, Contessina Cecia, Conte Sauro, Conte Stinco, who hadn't wished to be separated from his Galletto even on that occasion and had even ridden it up the stairway wearing his tails and had then hitched it to a trestle in a far corner of the room, and then Marchesa Daria and the twins, who in the end hadn't been persuaded by the wet nurse and had reshaped their ears, and everyone else. Marchesa Nivea was not there, unable to wake up, nor was Conte Vasco, who perhaps hadn't succeeded in getting out of bed or had been prevented by a more serious attack of asthma or by the Marchesa, and hadn't managed to put on his tailcoat, his moleskin cloak, and to take his rightful place at that sumptuous table, before his King.

All at once, from far away, from the henhouse, the horse whinnied. There was a sudden silence. The murmuring stopped. All heads turned toward the hall's great white gilded door.

The horse whinnied again, several times, indicating that someone had entered from the main entrance and then into the atrium that had to be crossed to reach the outer door of the stairway.

Indeed, a few seconds later, the bell rang.

In the room, everyone held their breath.

Someone crossed the anteroom as quick as lightning, began hurrying down the stairway, and it may well have been Piumetta who got there first since, even from where I was, the clank of her metal brace could be heard on the stone stairs.

Soon after, a sound of footsteps, slow, measured, solemn, that descended the stairway, then returned back up and across the anteroom toward the open doors of the dining hall.

The King entered. I couldn't see him. All I could glimpse, from time to time, when the mouth of the service hatch was free, was the boy who had come to prepare for his arrival and was the first to enter the hall, moving awkwardly, hunched, blushing at the sight of the guests all standing, rigid, in nervous anticipation. And Piumetta too, who hadn't managed to overcome the temptation of accompanying the King into the room, in front of everyone, before hopping away on her brace. But just a moment before she left I could distinctly see that an enormous hand belonging to someone outside my field of vision had taken one of her cheeks between two fingers and had pinched it, as adults do when they want to make a fuss over children, and that Piumetta recoiled in excitement and blushed, which meant that the hand must have belonged to the King, whom she had just escorted up the stairway.

From the steam-filled kitchen I didn't get a clear view of what was happening in the hall, because they kept pushing me away from the service hatch when they had plates to pass through or when the cook or one of her helpers left the stove and stuck her head inside, with an overwhelming curiosity to see the King.

"Goodness, what a hunk of a man!" one of them remarked, turning to the others.

"What a brute!" another added straightaway, he too sticking his head into the serving hatch.

The cook, her two helpers, and the girl who prepared the vegetables left the stove once more. They jostled with each other for a view.

"Hell, look at those hands!" the vegetable girl exclaimed. "They look like tennis rackets!"

"And how hairy they are!"

"And what a large head!"

"Enormous, bald . . . his head alone must weigh forty pounds!" the cook said.

"And his nose? Have you seen what a nose?"

"Looks like a boxer!"

Meanwhile, Piumetta appeared for a few moments in the kitchen, a gossip who always had something to say about everything.

"But sure! The King boxes!" she said, in answer to the one who had just spoken.

"He boxes?" the other asked. "The King's a boxer?"

"Sure!" Piumetta replied. "What's so strange about that! He has to keep in shape for when he can come back openly to his country. He trains each day with his servant . . . haven't you seen what a pancake that guy has in place of his nose?"

"And how do you know?" asked the cook, from the stove.

"I know!" Piumetta replied, vexed. "As a matter of fact he's promised to take me as his maid!"

"Oh yes? And when did he tell you that?"

"On the stairway!"

There was another shoving of heads and arms around the serving hatch. The hum of conversation from the hall was now building up, a sign that they had all relaxed after the great initial moment of tension and were talking at length with the King before sitting down at table. Even a few light bursts of laughter came through from time to time.

"Wow! Have you seen how he's looking down their cleavages?" said one of the cook's helpers maliciously.

Two or three heads peered through the hatch to see.

"He's fond of pussy!" the other assistant said.

There was an explosion of laughter in the kitchen.

"Keep your voice down, stupid!" said the cook, ticking him off with a naughty smile. "Or they'll hear out there!"

There was a sudden silence.

"Enough now!" said the cook, immersed in the steam, calling them back to work. "The King enjoys his food!"

"And his drink even more!" added Piumetta, who always

wanted to show she knew everything. "Why do you think his servant with the nose like a pancake came here day after day? He came to check out our food, our wines, he asked for a simple dinner, and plenty of it, with dishes from his own country, because he's tired of that sophisticated food he has to eat at courts around the world, at formal luncheons. He said he'll come into the kitchen in person afterward to thank the cook and all those who've prepared the meal, to dip his hands here and there into the cooking pots to taste the last leftovers stuck to the bottom . . ."

"Come off it!" someone had barely enough time to say.

A moment later, in the hall, a small bell rang, just once, to indicate that dinner was served.

There was a solemn silence while everyone took their places around their King. The fire burned in the fireplace. From the hall he could hear the sound of the logs crackling here and there, sending sparks into the chimney breast on which the coat of arms was painted. "What a shame Conte Vasco isn't here!" he kept thinking. "He in particular! Especially this evening! And Marchesa Nivea too, and her little voice . . . But she's always asleep, not even the sound of gunfire can wake her!"

More loud bursts of laughter were coming from the hall.

"Wow, he's certainly gorging himself!" said the boy responsible for putting serving dishes and soup tureens into the hatch and taking out the piles of empty plates that arrived from the other side. "He's stuffing down whole pumpkin tortelli, not even cutting them in half with his fork, groaning with pleasure, closing his eyes, making great gestures with his hand . . . And knocking back the drink!"

And indeed, empty wine bottles kept arriving at the serving hatch and were being replaced each time with new ones, though the dinner had only just begun.

"His servant's as red as a pepper," the boy continued. "He no longer knows where to look as he fills one glass after another, fast as he can, so the King won't lose his temper."

I had now given up watching, for I was so small that they pushed me aside as soon as I approached the hatch. I sat down on a small straw-bottomed chair not far away. From where I was, in those few moments when the hatch was clear, I could see only the section of table where the twins were sitting, turning their new faces in all directions so that everyone could see them, and stuffing whole tortelli into their newly cut mouths, and then risotto with pork ribs, pike with polenta, stuffed guinea fowl, braised vegetables, salad, cakes, as the dinner progressed and more and more empty bottles arrived and explosions of laughter grew ever louder.

"He's off!" said the vegetable girl, peering in with the excuse of handing through a platter. "He's telling a dirty joke!"

"A dirty joke? The King? The King himself?" someone complained.

"Why not!" the vegetable girl retorted. "He has no airs about him! He tells jokes, he's easygoing!"

"And what's he doing now?" the other asked.

"He's making rude propositions to Donna Paresi."

"To Donna Paresi?" the cook laughed from the other side of the kitchen. "Hah . . . he's chosen the right one there!"

"Yes, and what's more, he's even eyeing her tits!"

"And she?"

"She's gone as red as a beetroot, doesn't know where to put herself!"

Laughter. Someone was pouring dregs from the bottles that kept returning from the hall.

Then, from the other side, something was heard falling to the ground.

"What's happened?"

"The King has stood up with his glass in his hand. He's knocked his chair over. His servant's gone to pick it up."

"And why's he stood up?"

There was no time to reply because a moment later the King suddenly began to sing:

At tavern number one . . .

Everyone in the kitchen gave a look of amazement while the King on the other side kept singing that obscene song at the top of his voice and was even encouraging the other guests to join in.

At tavern number two . . .

But only the twins and Conte Stinco knew the words of the song and joined in.

"Have you heard?" said Piumetta, who had come into the kitchen for a moment, then went out again.

Meanwhile, on the other side, they had already reached "tavern number four." The King carried on singing at the top of his voice, pausing for a few moments now and then.

"He's wetting his whistle!" someone explained. "Singing is thirsty work!"

The King kept encouraging the other guests to join in the chorus.

"Even the ladies! Even the ladies!" he shouted, his voice slurred by wine.

But the ladies evidently didn't know the song and kept silent. A few seconds later, however, one female voice joined in, high, shrill, excited.

At tavern number five . . .

I shuddered slightly on my chair as I recognized the female voice that had joined in singing.

"It's Piumetta!" said the cook. "She's managed to sneak in even there. That child has no shame at all!"

In his excitement, the King was banging his fist on the table every so often, plates and glasses could be heard clattering.

At tavern number six . . .

At tavern number seven . . .

At tavern number eight . . .

Piumetta's voice rose higher and higher, almost drowning the King's with her high notes.

All of a sudden the singing stopped. There was a moment of deep silence.

You could have heard a pin drop.

An instant later, the King began another song, with a voice suddenly slow, serious, emotional, unrecognizable in the general silence.

"What's he singing?" someone near me asked quietly, almost in a murmur.

"It's the King's anthem!" the cook said.

The voice of the King continued singing alone. Then, one by one, all the voices of the noble guests, men and women, began to sing, joining together in a slow, solemn chorus that brought tears to the eyes.

Everyone in the kitchen stood still in silence.

One of the two helpers took a step forward, bent to look into the serving hatch.

"Now they're all standing round their King," he said, turning toward the others, "their faces all wet with tears. They're singing and crying."

The chorus continued, slow, solemn, growing louder, and I thought that maybe Conte Vasco could hear it from his room, from his bed, and was mouthing the words to himself, struggling to breathe, and that maybe even the little voice inside the Marchesa's frozen belly could hear it, and that maybe it too was secretly joining in, there inside, and that maybe even the hawk flying high in the sky over the court-yard was listening to it, flying quietly, not even flapping its wings so as not to disturb it with the rustling of its feathers in the deep darkness.

I couldn't say how long the singing lasted, for I had lost track of time. But I know that all at once, while everyone in the kitchen was standing still, in silence, with tears in their eyes, the door flew opened and suddenly the King came in, unsteady on his legs, staggering from the excess of wine.

He was tall, enormous, his belly stuck well out beneath his white dress shirt, lips purple, eyes glazed. He was stand-ing with difficulty, swaying. His servant was helping him to keep on his feet, propping him up with his body, holding him fastened to his waist, eyes lowered, red in the face.

In this way the King approached the cook, her two helpers, the waiter, the vegetable girl, asked each of them their name to thank them personally with his slurred voice, swaying.

"Tonight, my kingdom was here, my realm was here," he said, looking them all in the face. "And your King has eaten from your hands like a child."

He turned to leave and, in doing so, saw me, immobile, invisible, in my corner.

"And who are you, little one?" he suddenly asked me, as I stood, stock-still, in front of my little chair.

"I don't know," was all I could say, as the King was already leaving the kitchen and, as he passed, I thought he also whispered something in the ear of the vegetable girl, I couldn't say what, but I heard the girl whisper, blushing: "Your Majesty, what are you saying!"

I don't really remember what happened after that, or at what time the guests left, Conte Stinco with his Galletto, the King too, supported by his servant to make sure he didn't roll down the stairway. I don't remember what I did between this and when I went to sleep in my little bed, nor what happened while I was in bed, for I think I fell fast asleep and what happened after wasn't sleep but something like a sudden loss of consciousness. Nor do I know how long I remained like that in bed, I don't know whether I fell asleep or fainted, nor what time of the night it was when I suddenly heard a small, soft, agonizing call, as if something or someone was crying or screaming from some point infinitely deep, far away.

I woke at once.

"It's the little voice!" I suddenly realized.

I jumped down from the bed, put on my clothes, my shoes in a hurry because the little voice kept on screaming, screaming.

What happened after is almost impossible to describe. Nor can I say whether it lasted very long or whether it all happened in a short time. Can I manage to describe it? I'll try to carry on slowly, little by little, forcing myself to tell and solemnly recounting everything as though I were reliving it now.

So, now I'm standing. I've put my shoes on. I don't know whether I've managed to tie the laces, because the little voice keeps calling me, keeps calling.

I run into the blue room, rest my ear on the dome of the belly. But it's all filthy, wet! What's going on? The little voice is screaming, screaming loud. Why doesn't it wake the Marchesa? And yet she's in a deep sleep, or maybe in something more. The rest of the house seems fast asleep too, even though the little voice keeps screaming, screaming, screaming.

"Go and see! Go and see!" it screams from there inside. "Go and see!"

"Where? What?" I whisper, still numb with sleep or from fainting.

"Go and see! Go and see!" the little voice keeps screaming. "I hear everything from here, I know everything. Don't stay here. Go and look in the other houses too, in the courtyard. Go and see with your own eyes. There's been pandemonium tonight!"

I take a few steps toward the door, through the blue

room, the dark anteroom. I look out onto the stairway, switch on the light. I don't know whether it's my eyes, still half sleepy, that aren't seeing clearly, but it barely seems to illuminate the steps. And what is this terrifying stink? There are pieces of fresh excrement here and there on the stairs, on the carpet. "Maybe it was the cats," I tell myself. "Maybe they stuffed themselves with leftover food, maybe they·got diarrhea, messed the whole stairway . . ." But it doesn't seem like the usual smell of cat shit. "Maybe one of the guests felt ill, left their ordure on the stairway . . ." I think, confused.

I go out into the courtyard. A sound comes from high up. As though someone's waving a black flag in the sky. What can it be? I look up. But it's all black. I realize, from a shadow I see passing over me, that it's the hawk flying low over the mouth of the courtyard. Someone is sobbing somewhere. I move in that direction. It's the vegetable girl: she's lying on the ground, doubled up, close to the garbage pit, pressing both hands against the base of her stomach.

"What are you doing there on the ground?" I ask.

She makes no reply. She's crying, crying.

The horse starts neighing desperately, the sound of the hens can be heard, woken abruptly in the night, they are flapping terrified against the henhouse walls, ceilings. I have my heart in my mouth, not least because I've just glimpsed the outline of Conte Vasco in the shadows, standing still, in the darkness, at the door of his house, wearing his moleskin cloak.

"Conte Vasco!" I cry. "What are you doing standing there, outside, alone at this time of night! You'll catch cold!"

He makes no reply.

"What's going on?"

He makes no reply. He doesn't seem to hear me. I can hear only his breathing, like bellows, amplified by the silence, by the darkness, while his eyes stare in some direction, petrified.

The door behind him is open, the light is on. I go inside. It's all lit up, even though it's night. I hear crying. It's Marchesa Daria. I go past her. She doesn't even see me. The inside doors of the house are all open. I continue on. I put my head into the room of Contessa Mia and Contessa Sua. They are both lying facedown on the wooden floor, which is all wet. They are moving slightly, with their legs, their arms, in the wetness.

I run outside. I glimpse the outline of Galletto ripped to pieces on the inner pathway as I approach Conte Sauro's house. That is open too. I go in. It is all lit up, the doors are wide open. "Maybe it's always like this at night in this courtyard," I tell myself. "Maybe the lights are always on, the houses left open, so you can pass from one to the other, maybe they are all awake . . . Maybe it was just me who didn't know, since I've never been up at night, I've always been shut up in my little room, asleep."

There's no one in the kitchen. I go slowly up the stairway. I reach the drawing room, the yellow room. There are traces of blood here and there, on the upholstery, on the footstools. "Maybe the twins have been cutting themselves again!" I wonder.

I take the corridor toward the bed chambers. All the doors are wide open. It is flooded with light. But what are these cries? I see Donna Paresi pass in her nightgown. Her nightgown is bloodstained too, as well as those parts of her legs that stick out, her bare feet, her toes.

"Donna Paresi!" I call out. "I'm here! Don't you see me? What has happened?"

Not even she replies. She doesn't seem to hear me. There's moaning, crying, from every direction. I carry on. The twins' bedroom. Both are lying facedown on the bed, naked from the waist down, their buttocks stained with blood, with another thick, dark liquid that looks like petroleum. They are murmuring something to each other, crying. I come across Contessina Cecia. She's approaching along the corridor in a bathrobe torn all over, with bloodstained slippers.

"Cecia, little Cecia! What is it? What's happened?" I ask.

She doesn't answer either. She doesn't see me. She keeps repeating something with that giggle of hers, trembling. Conte Sauro is slumped across an armchair, his shirt torn, his nose all ripped open, bones sticking out, all covered with blood. Conte Stinco also lies motionless nearby, his teeth red, broken.

"And my friend," I suddenly think. "What has happened to my friend?"

I call him. I call him. I hear crying from somewhere. "I know!" I tell myself. "He's gone to hide on that small back staircase that leads to the roof. He's hiding up there, he's safe!" I know how to get there because he once took me to visit that secret refuge of his. He dragged an old mattress inside, pulled it up the stairs, put a little candle nearby as well, so he could see.

I slip through the trapdoor that leads to the back stairs, enter that hideout. Yes, that's it, and the little candle is still alight there by the stairs, and my friend is there on the mattress thrown down at the top of the stairs. But he's crying, he's crying. He's all filthy, wet. He doesn't see me. "Oh, no, no . . ." I tell myself. "He hasn't made it! He didn't manage to escape!" I go back down. I go down the main stairway. I come across the wet nurse, disheveled. Her mouth is a mess, she's been sick. She doesn't see me either, doesn't acknowledge me.

"No one sees me tonight," I tell myself.

I reach the courtyard. Conte Vasco is still there, in the dark, wrapped in his moleskin cloak, as if on guard, motionless, petrified. He is struggling to breathe. He sees nothing. He doesn't answer.

"Why doesn't anyone see me tonight?"

I go back to my house. I climb the main stairway. But just as I reach the top, heading toward my room, and then toward the little voice that is still calling me from the blue room, all of a sudden I hear a slow, rhythmic, frightening, metallic movement echoing up the stairway from behind. My breathing stops. My hair stands on end as I realize that this is the sound of Piumetta's leg brace slowly climbing the steps.

I turn around.

Yes, it's Piumetta. But she isn't laughing, isn't hopping. She's white as a sheet. She's mumbling something. I can't understand. I look down. There's a trail of blood behind her. It's trickling down from inside her little legs, from the metal brace. All the marble steps and the carpet are filthy.

I go back down.

"Piumetta!" I say. "What have they done to you?"

I'm not even sure she sees me. But she answers: "Down in the wood store . . . on the coal . . . he's still there!"

"He, but who?"

"The King."

I turn to go down, toward the hidden door of the wood store, painted like the walls of the stairway.

A moment later the door opens.

I run down.

"What have you done to Piumetta?" I shout at the King, who is coming out.

I look at him. He is pale, his mouth half open, his tongue swollen. A repulsive smell is coming from his unbuttoned coat with blackened edges.

He is looking at me. He staggers. His mouth distorts. He tries to sneer, but his lips can't manage to move. I don't know if he sees me, because his eyelids are heavy, almost closed. But he's mumbling with his voice slurred, belching:

"Ah . . . of course . . . you were there too! Hell, you got away from me!"

A second later, from the small door of the wood store, his servant appears too.

I turn toward him.

He looks back at me. His eyes are fixed, he is quietly crying.

My legs suddenly give way.

"And you, who are you?" I shout from somewhere on the ground.

He looks at me, his face all wet. He is crying.

"I . . . I . . ." he stammers.

I get up, run away, up the stairway.

"He can do whatever he wants!" Piumetta shouts at me, angrily, from above. "He's the King!"

"No, he's not the King!" I shout back at her, as I run up the stairway. "Haven't you understood yet? You who always know everything . . . The King is that other one!"

Piumetta bursts into loud tears, runs off, hopping on her brace, leaving a mess everywhere. The trail lengthens. Over the marble stairs, over the carpet.

She runs inside the house.

I carry on up, into the anteroom. The little voice is still screaming, screaming, screaming, in the farthest corners of the dark house.

I run into the blue room.

I stop at once, for I seem to glimpse an enormous presence in the half-light of the room.

"What's here, inside?" I ask, terrified.

The hawk has entered the house from one of the windows left open and is now perched on the great sphere of
Marchesa Nivea's belly, as if on a globe, and spreads its great
wings upon it in the darkness.

I can see its head thrust back, ready to attack her belly
with its beak, and to rip it open, and to go rummaging for
the frozen little body that is hidden there inside.

"Go away! Go away!" I shout, rushing toward it and
flapping my little arms.

The hawk turns its head to one side, in a plume of feathers. It stares at me with its round, wide, glassy eye.

But it doesn't move.

I run to grab Conte Alano's sword, pulling it down from
the wall.

I unsheathe it, whirl it in the air toward the hawk, which
flaps its enormous wings, once, twice, to intimidate me. I
keep whirling the sword against it, in the air stirred up by its
moving feathers.

All of a sudden the hawk takes off, unhooks its claws
from the belly, rises into the air, flying low, gigantic, heavy
toward the door, its vast wings colliding against ornaments,
pictures. It manages to pass through the door. I hear it flying and crashing about in the other rooms before heading

out over the filth-covered stairway, then leaving by the main entrance door, still open at the bottom, flying up from the courtyard, and taking its rightful place once again, high in the sky.

I drop the sword, move toward the belly. But it is all cold, wet, all smeared with blood, with froth.

"He came knocking at my watery door..." the little voice cries from inside. "He came inside with all his weight . . . and pushed, pushed, crushed me, split me open . . . His servant held the Marchesa's legs while the other one thrust into the frozen opening . . . Have you not yet understood? He has violated everyone, tonight, in here!"

"And why hasn't he violated me too?" I try asking the little voice.

"Because you're not there."

"I'm not here? Then where am I?"

"You're here!"

"There?"

"Yes, yes, you're here, with me. Your eyes are closed up too, creased up. I'm protecting you, I wrap my frozen little body around you to protect you from attack, from the cold, I'm the first to take the ice on top of me, I'm creating a niche for you, inside my frozen little body. You're not alone, here inside, there's another cold, wet little creature beside you. Where did you imagine you were? You're not there, you're still here, here with me. You're not yet born, but you will be born. And then, only after you are born, I too will be born.

I will be born for you. You have no one else but me. My frozen little eyes cannot form, my cold blood cannot feed my body. I will be born blind, deformed, undeveloped. I will be ugly and good. You will come to my bedside, I will stroke your head, I will listen to you, I will speak to you, I will comfort you. Here everything is cold, frightening, frozen. My cells, blood platelets . . . How can anyone be born in all this coldness? And yet you will be born. I'll let you go down first when the uterus starts to expand. First you and then me, first you and then me, first you and then me. I'll contract my little formless body that I have just described, I'll gather all my strength, I'll push you out with my frozen little feet . . . But you will be born, you will be born!"

Thank you all
for your support.
We do this for you,
and could not do
it without you.

DEEP
VELLUM

PARTNERS